LONG ROAD TO ABILENE: THE WESTERN ADVENTURES OF CADE MCCALL

Also by Robert Vaughan

LONG ROAD TO ABILENE: THE WESTERN ADVENTURES OF CADE MCCALL

ROBERT VAUGHAN

WOLFPACK PUBLISHING
LAS VEGAS

WOLFPACK PUBLISHING
— EST 2013 —

Wolfpack Publishing
6032 Wheat Penny Avenue
Las Vegas, NV 89122

ISBN 978-1-62918-984-0

1

Twin Creek Ranch, Howard County, Texas – 1927:

OWEN WISTER DROVE his Packard Six Sedan under the arch that spread over the driveway that led to the home of Cade McCall. The driveway, covered with white rocks, cut through the middle of a well-maintained lawn which was surrounded by a split log fence, festooned with climbing Paul's Scarlet roses.

There were several buildings on the grounds, including a barn, the machine shed, the bunkhouse, the ranch overseer's house.

The main house was relatively large, but not ostentatious. Compatible with the other structures, it was a two – story, white, clapboard house with a red roof and a single dormer window. The pillared porch stretched all the way across the front of the house, then wrapped around to the left side. There were a couple of swings on the porch, hung from the ceiling at right angles to afford congenial conversation for the occupants.

As the writer stepped from his car he was met by a very pretty young lady that he judged to be about nineteen. She was wearing a blue and white pull-on dress with a hemline that fell between her ankles and knees.

"Mister Wister?" She laughed. "I've been wanting to say that; 'Mister Wister' but then, I expect you have heard that a lot."

"Yes," Wister replied.

"I'm Amanda McCall. Grandpa is in the library. Come on, I'll take you to him."

"Thank you," Wister said. Reaching back into the car he removed a brown leather satchel.

Owen Wister had come to Twin Creek Ranch, the 60,000 acre cattle ranch in Central Texas, to interview Cade McCall, a man about whom more than a few books had been written. Because of his storied past, he had been portrayed on the movie screen by such actors as Gary Cooper and William S. Hart.

Wister was here because he planned to write a biography, The Western Adventures of Cade McCall, His Story, As told to Owen Wister.

There was an unpretentious entry foyer flanked by paintings. On one side was the portrait of a man who appeared to be in mid-forties, wearing a red shirt and dark vest. The painting on the other side of the foyer was that of an attractive woman, her head turned to one side in a pensive pose, the white silk blouse showing just enough of her neck to display a pearl necklace.

"That's grandma and grandpa, but then you know that," Amanda said when she saw where Wister was directing his gaze. "Weren't they good looking people then?"

"Well now, Darlin', are you saying we aren't good looking now?"

The man who asked the question was tall and rangy. At 84, he had a full head of silver hair, and a moustache that curled down around either side of his mouth. Just above his right eye was a pale, hook-shaped scar. His bright blue eyes were twinkling with amusement. He had just stepped through one of the doors that opened off the foyer.

"Why, no, grandpa!" Amanda insisted. "You were very handsome then, and you are very handsome now."

Cade McCall chuckled, then extended his hand. "Hello, Dan, it's been a long time." Cade's voice was deep, and resonant.

"Hello, Cade. Yes, it has been."

"Dan?" Amanda asked, confused. "Why did grandpa call you Dan? I thought your name was Owen Wister."

"Owen is my name, and the name I write under, but family and friends call me Dan." He smiled. "And ever since an adventure we once shared in Wyoming, I consider Cade a friend."

"Let's step into the parlor," Cade invited. "Amanda, get your grandmother and your mom and dad. I think I can convince Dan to play the piano for us."

"Oh! Do you play? I love the piano!" Amanda said.

"If Dan wasn't one of the best known novelists in America, he would be one of the best known musicians," Cade said.

"It's wonderful to see you again, Dan," Molly said as she embraced him. "I read 'The Right Honorable, The Strawberries' in COSMOPOLITAN MAGAZINE. I enjoyed it very much."

"Thank you. I'm working on a collection of short stories that I intend to call WHEN WEST WAS WEST. Though I'm going to give Cade an entire book, I've no doubt that some of his adventures will find their way into the collection."

"You have people like Bat Masterson, Wyatt Earp, and Wild Bill Hickock to draw from. And that's just the good guys. I don't see room for me in that crowd."

"Don't sell yourself short, Cade. Your name is equal to any of those you've mentioned."

"Yeah, well, why don't we all get seated?" Cade asked, uncomfortable with the accolades. "I'm anxious to get the concert started."

Once everyone had found a place, they turned their attention toward Owen Wister as he took his seat on the piano bench, and stared at the keyboard for a long moment. Then he began to play. The music, soft and melodic, rose from the soundboard filling the parlor with its resonance, and embracing the listeners with its beautiful strains.

"Oh, what is that piece?" Amanda asked when Wister finished the first number.

"That was CLAIRE DE LUNE, FROM THE SUITE BERGAMASQEBY, by Claude Debussy," Wister said.

Amanda chucked. "It's beautiful, but I don't have any idea what that means."

"It means the light of the moon, over the Italian town of Bergamo."

Wister played a few more pieces from various artists, then Cade stood.

"All right, folks, I know Dan didn't come here to give us a private concert, and I appreciate that he let me ambush him as I did. But he came here to work, so I think we should let him get started."

Amanda and the others were effusive in their delight of his music and they expressed their gratitude as they exited the parlor.

"How long do you plan to stay with us?" Cade asked.

"As long as it takes for me to write the book, or until you get tired of my hanging around, and kick me out and send me on my way," Wister replied. "Whichever occurs first."

Cade chuckled. "I reckon it'll be interesting to see which one that will be."

Wister joined him in laughter. "That it will," he agreed. "Come on, we'll talk in the library."

After they left the parlor, Wister looked around at the library, richly furnished, and with all four walls lined with thousands of books.

"You've done well for yourself, since the first time I met you," Wister said.

"And you are wondering how an old cowboy can afford such a place. Well, I filed on this land some time ago, and acquired most of it through homesteading. I also took advantage of some state grants during my intermittent times as a Ranger, and I bought some of the adjacent land when it came available.

"I got into raising Herefords while most of the other ranchers were still raising Longhorns. Herefords were like gold in the cattle market then, and, with Will as my partner, a good foreman, and good hands, we've managed to make a go of it."

"Considerably more than a 'go' I would say," Wister replied. "I saw several oil derricks, I expect that's brought in a few shekels as well."

"Oh yes, they have been quite lucrative. And thanks to Will, we've managed to keep the oil company at bay, providing us with enough space to still raise cattle."

"From the Cade McCall I know, I can see that would be a priority. Your good fortune has been well earned."

"I've had my ups and downs," Cade admitted. He held his arm out toward an area of the library where a large leather chair sat, as well as a sturdy oak desk with its own chair.

"We can sit over there," he said. "I expect you'll want to take notes, so you may use the desk if you wish, or sit in the chair or one of the sofas."

"Thank you," Wister said.

Wister chose the desk then removed from his satchel a tablet and several pencils.

"How's this going to work?" Cade asked as he settled into the leather chair. "Are you going to ask questions?"

"No, I'd rather you just start telling me your story."

"Where do you want me to start?"

"I know that you are from Clarksville, Tennessee. Why don't you start there?"

After a long day of taking notes, and asking questions to verify certain aspects of the story, Cade asked Wister if he would like to take a ride around the ranch. Wister agreed, thinking they might do so in Cade's car, but when they went outside, one of Cade's hands had two saddled horses waiting for them.

"You haven't gotten so citified that you can't ride anymore, have you?" Cade teased as he swung into the saddle.

"I think I can handle it, if you'll just show me where the clutch is."

Cade laughed, clucked at his horse, and the two of them rode out.

In his room that night, Wister began to consolidate his notes, forming them into the structure of the book he would be writing. This was, he knew, only a first draft. But with the first draft to provide the matrix, and the notes to provide the content, he began the project.

The Western Adventures of Cade McCall
His Story, As told to Owen Wister.
Owen Wister

Jonathan McCall's farm consisted of two hundred acres of good Tennessee bottomland, laid out along the east bank of the Cumberland River. The farm was four miles southwest of Clarksville, which was Tennessee's first incorporated city. Jonathan lived on the farm with his wife, Margaret, and his two sons, Cade and Adam.

That bucolic existence came to an end, however, with the outbreak of the Civil War . . .

2

Clarksville, TN – April, 1862:

CADE MCCALL WAS NINETEEN, but he had done a man's work since he was twelve. As a result, his six foot, one inch frame displayed wide shoulders, and muscular arms. His hair was more rusty than red, and his eyes were a deep blue.

Cade's brother, Adam, was three inches shorter, but because he did the same work, he was no less muscular. Cade, Adam, their father and mother, were having a discussion over the supper table.

"I see no reason why you should have to go," Margaret said. Margaret was Cade's mother. "It isn't our war, we don't have any slaves. You boys have worked your whole lives alongside Julius and Effie, and we pay them and furnish them a house."

"Mama, they just fought a big battle at Shiloh," Cade said. "Half of that battle was fought in Tennessee. It is our war."

"Yes," Adam added. "And there were hundreds, probably thousands of Tennessee men killed in that battle. And I don't expect very many of them owned slaves either."

"I am aware of that," Margaret said as tears slid down her cheeks. "Don't you see? I just don't want either one of you to wind up being one of those boys lying dead on the battlefield."

Jonathan, the boys' father, reached over to lay his hand gently on Margaret's shoulder.

"Margaret, don't you realize that those boys lying there dead are the sons of other mothers and fathers, who loved them no less than we love our boys?"

"What are you saying, Jonathan? Are you saying that you agree with Cade and Adam, that you want them to join the army?"

"No, I don't want them to join the army. I would prefer that they stay home, help manage the farm, and sometime soon maybe buy some of Mr. Byrd's land so they can each have farms next to us. I want Cade to marry Melinda, and give us grandchildren, but, we don't always have the things we want. Sometimes God puts other things in our way, and we'll just have to deal with it the best we can. This isn't the first war that sons have gone off to fight, and it won't be the last."

"You're saying let them go."

"I'm saying we can't stop them, nor should we try."

"Thanks, Pop," Cade said.

"Hey, how about me?" Adam asked. "You've already got Cade married to Melinda, who am I going to marry?"

Cade laughed, and reached over to muss the hair of his younger brother. "Who, in their right mind, would marry you?" he teased.

"Ha, you don't know. I might get a girl of my own, some day," Adam replied, joining in the laughter.

"What about Melinda?" Margaret asked. "Have you told her?"

Cade was quiet for a moment.

"You haven't told her, have you?"

"I'm going to tell her tonight," Cade replied, his voice so low as to barely be heard.

The moon, reflecting on the surface of the Cumberland River, sent forth little slivers of silver, to compete with the golden flashes of hundreds of fireflies. Cade and Melinda were sitting on a blanket that had been spread out on the bank of the river.

"Papa said he would help us buy some of Mr. Byrd's land," Melinda said.

Cade picked up a rock and tossed it into the river. The concentric circles working out from the rock disturbed the silver of the moon. He didn't answer Melinda's comment.

"I know, I know, you're too proud to accept anything from papa, but remember, it'll be my farm too. I mean, if we are husband and wife, won't it?"

"Melinda, maybe we should wait," Cade finally said.

"Wait? What do you mean, wait? Wait for what?"

"There's a war on."

"I know there's a war on, but what does that have to do with us?"

"It has everything to do with us, Melinda." He pointed to the river. "Right now the Yankees control this river. Why, they could put a gunboat right out there and start shelling Clarksville, and there wouldn't be anything we could do about it.

"It's up to us. I can't just sit by and let the Yankees take over everything I've ever known . . . everything I've ever loved."

"I thought you loved me."

"I do. When I said, everything I've ever loved, I'm talking about you."

"So, what you are saying is, you don't want to marry me."

"Yes, I do want to marry you, more than anything in the world. But Melinda, I can't do it now. I can't go off to war and leave a wife behind me. Why, there'd only be half of me, and half of you. If you love me, you will wait for me. We'll get married when the war is over and I've come back home." Cade smiled, then put his finger under her chin. "Why, I'll even let your papa help us out in buying the farm."

Melinda took Cade's hand in hers, then raised it to her lips and kissed it. "Oh, Cade, I don't see anything good coming from this. I . . . I have the most awful feeling that you won't be coming back."

"I'll be back," Cade promised her. "Why, I don't expect this war will last more than six more months, a year at the most."

Franklin, TN - 29 November, 1864

Over the last two and one half years, Sergeant Cade McCall had fought at Antietam with the 1st Tennessee. Then, with the 33rd Tennessee he had fought at Perryville, Stone's River, Chickamauga, Chattanooga, Ringgold Gap, and Kennesaw Mountain. Now, just outside Franklin, he lay stretched out near a big black kettle sitting over the fire that had been built from collected fence stakes. There was a flash of light on the horizon, followed somewhat later by a low, rumbling sound. The uninitiated might think it was thunder, but after over three years of war, Cade could tell the difference between cannon fire and thunder.

With each firing, a flash of light would light up the night horizon, followed by the sound of the gun. Cade counted fifteen seconds between the flash and the bang, which meant that the guns were three miles away.

"Glad they aren't shootin' toward us," Adam said.

"I don't care if they are or not, I don't plan on leavin' this spot 'till the soup is done," Gordon Waters, said.

This evening Cade, his brother Adam, and the others of General Alexander Stewart's Third Corps, had enjoyed the good luck to have been bivouacked in what proved to be a most propitious location.

"Taters!" one of the soldiers shouted shortly after they had arrived. "Look here, fellers! We got taters!"

"Yeah, they're all over the place!" Another shouted, and for the next several minutes the soldiers forgot all about war and concentrated on uncovering the mounds of unharvested potatoes. When they were issued their rations, which consisted of fresh pork, the twenty soldiers in Cade's mess immediately decided to put their individual rations together to make a soup. All the others of the Third Corps came to the same agreement, and now, the smell of a hundred or more cooking pots blanketed the area with a rich aroma that enticed the tastebuds.

"Hey, Cade, now that you've just been made a sergeant and all, that doesn't mean you're goin' to start givin' me orders, does it?" Adam asked. "I mean like, do this, or do that."

"Come on, Adam, you know how it is," Cade said. "Just because we are brothers, that doesn't mean I can play favorites. I have to treat you just like I treat everyone else. Besides," he added with a chuckle. "I've outranked you for your whole life."

"You've been one year older than me for my whole life, you haven't outranked me," Adam insisted.

"Sounds to me like he outranks you," Waters said with a chuckle. "But he doesn't outrank me."

"What do you mean, I don't outrank you? I'm a sergeant, you're a corporal."

"Uh huh. I'm also Melinda's brother, and if you don't treat me right, I'll just tell her not to marry you."

"Ha!" Cade said. "When has Melinda ever listened to you?"

"I don't know why she would listen to either one of you," Adam said.

"You do remember the time the two of you dunked her hair into that ink bottle, don't you?"

"That was a long time ago," Cade said.

"Yeah, well, I haven't forgot, 'n it's for sure, she hasn't forgotten it either."

"How's that soup comin'?" Pogue Elliot, one of the other soldiers asked.

Clint Copley had volunteered to do the cooking, and he stuck his bayonet down into the soup to test one of the potatoes.

"Damn, Copley, you ain't never stuck a Yankee with that bayonet, have you?" Pogue asked.

"Yeah, I have, but you don't need to be worryin' none about it. I wiped it clean on my pants," Copley replied, easily.

"Oh, well then I'm sure that makes it all right," Cade said, and the others laughed.

"It's ready," Copley said.

A few minutes later, all the men of A Company were sitting around, enjoying what most agreed was the best meal any of them had eaten in several weeks, even if they didn't have any salt. Cade, Adam, Gordon, Pogue, and Copley found a flat rock and they were using it as a table.

"You know what? I've always known that you and Melinda would get married someday," Gordon said.

"What makes you say that?"

"Because when she was just a little girl, she told me that when she grew up she was going to marry you."

Pogue laughed. "Yeah, little girls is like that. They put it in mind who they're goin' to marry long a' fore a boy will ever start thinkin' 'bout such a thing. I got three sisters, so I know."

"Are you goin' to buy some land from Byrd, 'n farm after you 'n sis get married?" Gordon asked.

"I expect I will," Cade said. "I don't know how to do anything but farm."

"Well, I'll tell you this, you're pretty damn good at killin' Yankees," Copley said. "That's how you made sergeant."

"Yeah, well, once the war is over, I don't think someone could take up killing Yankees as an avocation," Cade replied.

"I reckon not," Copley said with a little chuckle.

"You ever think about it?" Gordon asked.

"Think about what? Killing Yankees?"

"Well, yeah, I guess so. But, what I really meant is, do you ever think about getting killed?"

"Sometimes I do, yeah," Cade answered. "I mean, how can you not think about it? But, as much as possible, I try not to."

"I wonder what it's like," Adam asked. "Do you think it hurts?"

"Well, hell yeah, it has to hurt," Pogue said. "You've seen as many men kilt as I have. I mean, how's it not goin' to hurt to have a big, gaping hole in your body?"

"It seems to me like most have died quick and quiet," Copley said.

"How do you know they were quiet? With all the guns goin' off, 'n all the yellin' 'n such, they could be screamin' to high heaven 'n we wouldn't even hear them." Pogue finished his long comment with another spoon of soup.

"I wonder if you know when you're dead," Adam asked.

"What do you mean?" Gordon replied.

"I mean, say you get killed, would you be able to look down at your body and say, 'Damn, I'm dead?'"

"You'd have to still be hanging aroun' the battlefield to do that," Gordon said.

"Of course you would. How else would you be able to see yourself?"

"Well, there you go then," Pogue said. "Once I'm dead, I damn sure ain't plannin' on a' hangin' around where I was killed."

"Where would you go?" Gordon asked.

"I know where I'd go," Copley said. "I'd most likely go back home 'n see ma 'n pa 'n my sisters." He laughed. "Then, what I'd do is haint my sisters, just to get even with 'em for all the pesterin' they done to me for my whole life."

"I'd go to Paris," Gordon said. "I've always thought I'd like to see Paris."

"Not me. No way you'll ever get me on a ship," Adam said. "What if I was to be out in the middle of the ocean, and the ship happened to sink 'n ever' one drowned?"

Cade laughed. "You couldn't drown, dummy, you'd already be dead."

"Yeah, but I'd wind up being out in the middle of the ocean just stranded there."

"If you are a spirit, you can go anywhere," Cade said. "You wouldn't need a ship; all you would have to do is think about it, and there you would be."

"Yeah," Gordon said. "That's right, isn't it? All you'd have to do is think about it. That will really be somethin', won't it?"

"Damn, Gordon, you sound almost like you're lookin' forward to gettin' kilt," Copley said.

"No, don't get me wrong now, I'm not lookin' forward to it," Gordon replied. He was silent for a long moment. "But I've got a feeling I'm going to get killed pretty soon now."

"Ahh, don't be silly," Cade said, dismissively. "The five of us have been through almost three years of war, and nothing has happened to us yet. We didn't come this far to get ourselves killed now. Besides, I want all of you standing right there alongside Adam, watching, when Melinda and I get married."

"Cade's right," Jeter Willis said. "Quit thinkin' like that 'n enjoy this soup that Copley made. How long has it been, anyway, since any of us have had anything this good to eat?"

"Yeah," Adam said with a slow grin. "Yeah, Jeter's got that right. How come we're talkin' like this, instead of eatin'?"

The talk of dying passed, and they all began telling funny stories on each other, and on friends, so that the dinner became an enjoyable interlude in the midst of battle, not only because of the good food, but also because of the camaraderie of men who had been through so much together.

Long Road to Abilene

3

EARLIER THAT SAME DAY, they had run the Federals out of Columbia, and they had been told by their company and regimental commanders that it was General Hood's intention to retake Nashville. But to reach Nashville, they would have to go through Franklin, and General John Scholfied's XXIII Corps of the Army of the Ohio had heavily fortified Franklin, with reinforced breastworks.

"You think there'll be fighting tomorrow?" Gordon asked.

"I expect there will be," Adam said.

"You can count on it," Cade added. "General Hood isn't goin' to be satisfied until he's standing on the capitol steps in Nashville. He is one fighting son of a bitch, I'll tell you."

"Yeah, he's done lost an arm 'n a leg, 'n he could most likely just give it up 'n go home, but he won't do it," Copley said.

"He's still got his arm, he just can't use it," Pogue said. "Anyhow, why would he go home? It ain't like he's goin' to be up front with us when the fightin' starts."

"He won't, huh?" Cade asked.

"No, Generals most usually send us in to do the fightin'
while they stay behind," Pogue insisted.

"If that's the case, then tell me, Pogue, how it is that
General Hood lost his leg, and the use of his arm?"

Pogue was quiet for a moment. "I don't know. Yeah, I
guess some generals are up front with the men," he admitted.

"I don't know how you can say that, anyway. You know
as well as I do that General Stewart and General Cleburne are
always up front."

"Yeah, well, I sure wouldn't be if I was a general," Adam
said. "I'd be standin' in the back, pointing and waving, and
yelling, 'ya'll get 'em boys!' And then I'd just watch the
battle through field glasses."

"You'd watch through field glasses?" Cade asked, with a
smile.

"Yeah. Have you ever seen a general that didn't have
field glasses?" Adam replied.

"Well, there you go, Cade," Gordon said. "Find yourself
a real nice pair of field glasses, and you can forget about
being a sergeant. Why, more 'n likely General Lee would
make you a general.

"*Tell me, Colonel,*" Gordon said speaking in a voice that
he assumed mimicked General Lee's voice. "*Who is that fine
looking young sergeant down there with those field glasses?*

"*Why, general, that would be Sergeant Cade McCall,*"
Gordon said switching voices.

"*You go get that young man and bring him to me. Since
he has those field glasses, he isn't a sergeant anymore. Now
he's a general.*"

The others laughed at Gordon's impression of a
conversation between General Lee and an unnamed colonel.

"That sounds good, but most generals have to come from
West Point," Cade said.

"You mean if I had gone to West Point, I would be a
general?" Adam asked.

"That ain't hardly likely, Adam. Don't forget, the rest of us have seen you soldier," Gordon teased. "I don't think you would be made a general if you had a pair of field glasses and you had graduated from West Point."

"Speaking of West Point, did you know that General Hood and General Scholfield were roommates when they were at West Point?" Cade asked.

"How do you know that?" Copley asked.

"I overheard Colonel Hill and Captain Hanner talking about it. Colonel Hill went to West Point, so I figure he should know."

"I reckon, bein' as you're a sergeant now, you'll be overhearin' a lot of high-falutin' talk like that," Adam said.

"Oh, I expect I will," Cade replied.

"Damn, that's really something when you think about it, isn't it?" Gordon said. "I mean here these two men lived together in the same room, and now they're tryin' to kill one another. Why, that would be like us shooting at one another."

"Sergeant Cosgrove has a brother in the Yankee army," Cade said. "But at least they haven't run across each other yet."

There was enough soup that they all went back for seconds, but even as Cade and the others were cleaning their mess kit, Adam went back a third time.

"Damn, Adam, don't you ever fill up?" Gordon asked.

"I can always find room for a little more," Adam replied. "I look at it this way. What if some Yankee shot me dead, tomorrow? Why, I'd hate to go meet my Maker knowing that I had left some soup behind that I hadn't eaten yet."

Cade laughed. "I suppose that's as good a reason as any to have a third bowl of soup."

"Say, Cade, you got a letter from Melinda, today, didn't you?" Gordon asked.

"Yes."

"Are you goin' to read it to us?"

"What? Hell no, I'm not goin' to read it to you. Why should I? It's a personal letter."

"It might be personal, but you forget, she's my sister. I got a right to know what my own sister says, don't I?"

Cade smiled. "Not what she says to me, you don't."

Adam returned with his third bowl of soup, "I know what she said." He slipped into falsetto. "Oh, Cade, I love you so much."

"If you all already know what she said, why should I bother to read it?" Cade asked.

The others laughed.

The temperature dipped down into the high thirties during the night, and more than a thousand campfires were lit to push back some of the chill. There was no need for light discipline; General Scholfield's army already knew that Hood's army lay before them. The Confederate commanders urged that as many fires be built as could be sustained by the available fuel, believing that the great number of fires, indicating such a large body of troops, would have the effect of unnerving the Federals.

Cade, Adam, Gordon, Copley, Willis and Pogue, as well as the fifteen other men of their "mess" had put their blankets down around one of the fires, lying feet to the center, in order to make room for the maximum number of men to share the heat. Cade lay there, listening to the cracking of the fire, as well as the snores of the sleeping, watching the red sparks riding the heatwaves up to join with the blue stars in the dark sky. He was unable to sleep, his mind filled with thoughts evoked by the conversation that he and the others had over supper.

"One of the first things you have to put out of your mind," Cade always told the new recruits, *"is the idea that you might get killed. You have to become a fatalist about it. Why if it's your time, you could be plowing a field, and get kicked in the head by a mule."*

That's what Cade told the men who would be seeing battle for the first time, doing so to comfort himself as much as to comfort the neophytes. Thousands of men were bedding down tonight, both Union and Confederate, and Cade knew that for many of them, this would be their last night on earth. He thought of what Melinda had told him the night he announced that he was going to war.

"Oh, Cade, I don't see anything good coming from this. I . . . I have the most awful feeling that you won't be coming back."

Would this be his last night? Damn Gordon for speaking out loud the fears all had to face.

To put such thoughts out of his mind, Cade reached down into his tunic pocket and took out the letter he had received earlier. Sitting up, he turned and put his back to the fire, so there would be enough light for him to be able to read. Before he read a line, though, he held the little lock of hair, the tresses held together with a small, gold strand. The lock of hair had arrived with the letter.

Dear Cade,

I am sending you a chevelure. That's French for lock of hair. I want you to keep it, and that way a part of me will always be with you.

Mary Beth and her beau got married last week, then he went back to the war. I wish we had gotten married before you went back. You said you didn't want to make me worry about you if you were my husband. Oh, Cade, dear Cade, do you think I worry about you any less because we aren't married?

I love you so much. Did you not know that when we were quite young, and I got a briar in my foot so that you had to carry me home, that I was so happy to be in your arms that there was no sting from the needles of the briar? It was then that I knew I was in love with you, but I couldn't tell you, because you were too young.

I am sure that you are laughing at my declaration that you were too young, since you are a year older than I am. But souls have ages, as well as the body. I think that a woman's soul ages more quickly than a man's soul, and it was that old soul, in the body of a young girl, that fell in love.

I pray, nightly, that you be kept safe. You will have my love, always.

Sincerely,

Melinda

Reading Melinda's letter brought comfort to him. Holding this very piece of paper, the page Melinda had also held, was almost as if she were right here with him.

He lifted the little lock of hair to his nose and sniffed it, then he stuck it down into his pocket.

"Goodnight, Melinda," Cade said, speaking so quietly that his words were covered by the distant thump of artillery, and the more instant, and sharper crack of a gas bubble, trapped in a piece of wood that was being consumed by the fire.

4

CADE'S DIVISION was placed on the extreme right of the Columbia and Franklin Pike, making it the right wing of the front line of battle. The remainder of General Hood's troops were formed in successive lines, one behind the other.

"Lookie there," Pogue said, pointing in front of them.

There, across the field that separated the two armies, Cade could see several of the defenders, officers he assumed, standing on the breastworks, their blue uniforms clearly visible in the light of a sunny, November afternoon.

Before them was of a battery of thirty-six cannon on the main line of the Federal works. A little to the right of this main battery were six more pieces of artillery and these guns, Captain Hanner's company had been told, would be their objective. In addition, to the left, were eight more cannon.

How, Cade wondered, were human beings, armed only with pistols and rifles, expected to assault fifty cannon that would be firing grape and canister?

Although Cade formed the question in his mind, he didn't put voice to it because he knew that everyone else was thinking the same thing.

A number of mounted officers rode out in front of the formed battle lines. They were Generals Walthall, Loring, Cheatham, Quarles, Granberry, and Cleburne. The officers were holding a conference of some sort and, though they were too far away for Cade to hear, he could see them pointing to the enemy lines, then back to their own lines, then to the Federal artillery.

"Look at all them gen'ruls," Jeter Willis said. "They see all them Yankee cannons, 'n they know sure as we do, that we're a' fixin' to get ourselves chewed up like runnin' pork through a meat grinder."

"Quiet in the ranks," Cade said. He gave the order because such talk would be demoralizing for the others. He knew that, because it was demoralizing for him.

Cade, because he was a sergeant, stood slightly in front of the men under his charge, and he turned to look at his brother. Adam smiled, and nodded at Cade, who returned the nod.

Cade had faced death many times over the last two and a half years, and as he stood here now, waiting for the orders to advance across this open field, a calmness came over him. He might well be killed today, but then, everyone died, it was just a matter of when . . . and once you were dead, it didn't really matter when you died. It was a prospect he faced with more acceptance than fear.

He knew he could not explain this calm acceptance to anyone who had never before experienced it, and he knew, also, that he wouldn't have to explain it to anyone who had experienced it.

"Forward!" General Cleburne shouted, circling his hand over his head, then bringing it down to point toward the Yankee lines.

Holding his rifle with the bayonet pointed toward the Federal redoubts, Cade started across the field, part of a wave of thirty thousand men. Thirty thousand men couldn't be stopped, could they?

When they reached the first of the two Yankee lines, it looked as if the attack would prevail. They swept over the trench, killing or routing the defenders. The Yankees turned and ran toward the second line of defense.

"Keep on 'em!" Cade shouted to his men. "Keep as close as you can! We'll follow them right into their lines!"

The Confederate troops blazed away, staying so close to the Yankees they were pursuing that they were able to club them down without wasting ammunition. Excited yells of triumph rose from the throats of the attackers, and Cade saw, ahead of him, General Cleburne, leaning down from his saddle to slash the retreating Federals with his sword.

Then, suddenly, it all changed.

The fifty Yankee cannon opened fire. Double-loaded with grape and canister, many of the guns were in enfilade, and the storm of hot steel swept men down like wheat before a scythe.

Cade had thought that by maintaining close contact with the enemy it would provide them with some protection from the Yankee cannon, but he was wrong. The Federal gunners did not differentiate between the Confederates and their own men. They fired into the mass of human bodies, delivering unbelievable carnage.

In addition to that was the fire of the rifleman along the parapet. The storm of missiles was so intense that scores of men were literally blown away, but the Tennesseans would not give up. While some sought shelter in the outside, others worked their way west along the line. Here, there was great confusion and disorder. Cade and his yelling troops jumped over the parapet. Added to the other Confederates already there, they begin fighting with a reckless fury. It became a great swelling mob of men, engulfing everything in front of it along the nearly sixty-five yards between the retrenched line and main earthworks east of the Columbia Pike.

Desperately, some of the Tennesseans captured a Yankee battery and attempted to fire the gun into the Federal ranks. It was the focal point of the crisis, a crucial point where momentum tottered precariously and the battle might be won or lost. But the captured cannon couldn't be fired without friction primers, and when the Yankee gunners had run away they removed the primers and the lanyards. In the confusion of the moment, none could be found amid the debris. Some of the men broke open musket cartridges and poured powder into the vent tubes, thinking that by lighting the powder they might fire the cannon by hand.

Before they were able to do this, however, a surging wall of blue smacked into the Confederate ranks. For five minutes it was a hand-to-hand combat. Bayonets, clubbed muskets, revolvers, broken gun stocks, even bare hands became the weapons of the moment. A Yankee officer who had broken his sword picked up a hatchet and brought it down on the head of Gordon Waters. Gordon's blood and brains were splattered over Cade.

"No!" Cade shouted in shock, rage, and sorrow. Cade shot the Yankee officer in the face, and even after he was down, Cade bashed in his head with the butt of his rifle. This was no longer Tennessee, this was hell!

Like the men in his command, General Cleburne was now on foot, his horse having been shot from under him. "Follow me, men!" he shouted, waving his saber above his head and leading the way. Cade and the others disengaged from the useless, captured cannon in response to the general's call, but the smoke was so thick that the enemy's works could barely be seen.

The objective was the cotton gin. There, the Federal ranks were five or six men deep, with those in the rear loading and passing the muskets to those at the front to fire. Behind these men was a second rank waiting with loaded rifles. By now the ditch was so filled with dead that Cade crossed it by walking on the bodies. Only a few feet of earth separated the combatants, and the contest became most desperate

At about 40 yards from the works, and nearly in front of the salient at the cotton gin, in one shocking moment, a Minié ball struck just below and to the left of General Cleburne's heart, shredding veins and arteries like tissue paper as it ripped through his body. With his saber firmly gripped in his hand, he fell, the front of his gray tunic covered with blood.

"They killed the General!" Clint Copley shouted, but those words were no sooner out of his mouth that he was struck in the head and fell dead alongside the general. Now Gordon and Copley were gone and Cade looked around to see if he could locate Adam. He had been side by side with Jeter Willis the last time Cade saw him, but now neither Adam nor Jeter were anywhere to be seen.

The greatly depleted line reached the abatis where the defenders, now following the pre-determined tactic of final defensive fire, were cutting down attacking rebels and fleeing Yankees without discrimination. One of the Yankee soldiers, having been killed by his own men, fell in front of Cade. Cade had just fired his rifle and the fallen Yankee had two charged and capped pistols, so Cade reached down to pick them up. As soon as he did, two Federal soldiers stood up behind the works, and Cade killed both of them, one with each pistol.

Now the Confederates were at the base of the rampart, sticking their weapons into the small space between the earthen mound and the head-log to fire. The Yankees, without showing themselves, were holding their rifles out over the top of the head-log, shooting straight down. Cade saw Pogue lash out with his bayonet to slice off the hand of one of the defenders.

Reloaded, now, the Yankee cannon let loose another barrage of grape and canister, again mowing down Rebels by the score.

The ravings of the mangled soldiers on both sides of the parapet where frenzied and heartrending. Crazed by pain, many had no idea what they were yelling. Cade heard some of the men shouting, "Cease fire! Cease fire!" as if by so ordering, they could bring about the result.

Within the Confederate ranks all continued to be chaos as the blast of canister from the Yankee cannon piled dead men in front of the works. At one point there were so many bodies heaped around the guns that the dead literally had to be dragged aside to clear the muzzles so the guns could be fired.

Despite the terrible fusillade, Cade and the others continued their assault, some attempting to squeeze through the narrow openings in the earthworks. Through it all, the guns continued to fire double and triple canister at point-blank range.

Cade saw Andy Pearson pick up a loose timber from the works and start toward one of the cannon. Andy was only fifteen years old, a drummer boy who, after beating the long roll was supposed to drop back to the rear when the actual fighting started.

"Andy, no!" Cade shouted. "Get back!"

Andy either didn't hear Cade's shout, or chose to ignore it, and reaching the Yankee cannon, he jammed the loose timber from the earthworks into the gun's muzzle. But the cannon was already loaded, and the Yankee gunner jerked the lanyard. Andy was directly in front of the muzzle, and the muzzle blast distributed his bloody body parts in a ghastly rain.

"Cap'n Hanner! Sir, we have to surrender!" one of the soldiers shouted. "We are being slaughtered here!"

"Who has a white handkerchief?" Hanner called.

"I'm wearin' a white shirt under this," Pogue said.

The exchange had to be shouted, because of the noise of gunfire.

"Let me have it!"

Cade saw Captain Hanner tie a piece of the white shirt on a ramrod and lift it up. Then there was a huge explosion just to his right, and everything went black.

* * *

Adam McCall lay in bed, listening to the quiet now. The roar of guns and the screams and cries of dying and wounded men were just on the other side of his awareness. He looked through the hospital window out onto a Nashville scene that was dominated by men who were wearing Yankee blue.

"How are we doing this morning, Private McCall?"

Turning away from the window, Adam saw Dr. Barnes. The doctor was a surgeon in the Confederate army and, like Adam, was now a prisoner of war. But the Yankees had pressed the doctor into service, tending to the many Confederate wounded, a job he willingly accepted.

"If you mean my leg, it's not bothering me all that much," Adam said. "But there's nothing about the rest of me that's good."

"I know, I know, being a prisoner of war, even in a hospital, is not a very pleasant thing. But compare your situation with that of over two thousand of our boys who were killed in the battle. Why, we lost six generals, did you know that?"

"I know General Cleburne was killed, because I saw that," Adam replied.

"It wasn't just Cleburne. Generals Drake, Hill, Granbury, Gist, and Strahl were also killed," the doctor said.

"And so was my brother," Adam said.

"Yes," Dr. Barnes said. "I was told that your brother had been killed. Please forgive me, McCall, for carrying on about how many generals we lost, when you are still mourning your own brother."

"Like you said, Doctor, there were two thousand who were killed. I can't dwell on just one of them."

Suddenly, and unexpectedly, the glum expression of Dr. Barnes's face was replaced with a smile.

"On the other hand, I do have some good news for you," the doctor said. "As a matter of fact, you could call it outstanding news!"

"It's hard to see how any news could be good now. What is this good news you're talking about?"

"The Yankees are giving a lot of the wounded paroles. You're going home."

"What? They're just going to turn me loose, like that? I don't believe it. They want something from me, don't they?"

"All they want from you is your promise not to take up arms against them anymore."

"You mean just go home, and sit the rest of the war out?"

"Yes."

Adam was quiet for a moment, then he nodded. "All right," he said. "I'll do it. I wonder . . ."

"You wonder what?"

"I wonder if mom and pop have been told about Cade. I pray that they have been told. I don't want to be the one who will have to tell them."

"Whether they have been given the news or not, be thankful for this. You are alive, and you will be there to comfort them," Dr. Barnes said.

5

Chicago, *IL:*

THE TRAIN THAT HAD COME north all the way from Nashville consisted of two locomotives, a passenger car occupied by forty Union soldiers, and fifteen cattle cars, each car filled with one hundred Confederate prisoners of war. At the tail end of the train there was another passenger car, this one with forty Union soldiers who were guards for the prisoners.

It was cold on this December afternoon, and the wind came through the open spaces between the slats on the four sides of the car. But because the car was crowded with men who hadn't bathed in a long time, and, because of the smell of feces and urine, there being no facilities for the men to relieve themselves, the fresh air compensated for the cold. The fact that there were so many of them crowded into the car had the beneficial effect of providing some warmth to counteract the cold.

There was barely room to sit in the cattle cars, let alone lie down. To accommodate this, the prisoners worked out a schedule among themselves which allowed them to sleep in shifts for the three days they were in route to the Camp Douglas Prison on the shore of Lake Michigan.

"Did you see my brother die?" Melinda asked.

"Yes. I'm sorry. Gordon was a good man, and a good friend," Cade answered.

"How was he killed?"

"It was quick." Cade made no mention of the blood and brains spilled by the hatchet wielded by the Yankee officer.

"They say that Gordon died bravely and that he is a hero."

"Yes, that is true."

"I would rather have a live brother, than a dead hero."

"So many were killed in that battle," Cade said. "I was almost killed, the bomb burst so close to me."

Melinda ran her finger over the ridge above Cade's eye. "You have no eyebrows," she said.

"They were burned off in the explosion. They'll grow back."

Her fingers moved from a denuded eyebrow ridge up to his forehead where they hovered over a scar that rose, like a purple fishhook, just above the right eye.

"Does it hurt?" she asked.

"Not anymore. But I expect I'll have the scar for the rest of my life."

"That's all right, I will always love you, even with the scar, and whether you have an eyebrow or not. I know what! You can use the lock of hair I sent you, as an eyebrow."

"Yes, I could do that, couldn't I?"

Cade and Melinda were sitting in "their place" on the bank of the Cumberland River.

"Oh, Cade, why didn't we get married before you left? Now look. I am at home, without you, and you are on a train, going to a prison camp in Chicago."

"No!" Cade said. "I'm here, with you! Can't you see?"
He wanted to lay his hand on her cheek, but found that he
was quite unable to lift his arm.
"Melinda!" he called.
He saw Melinda's lips moving, and heard her voice. "I
will always love you . . . love you . . . love you."

The train hit a rough section of track and the cattle car
jerked severely enough to awaken Cade. For just an instant,
he was caught between the dream and the reality. He wasn't
with Melinda at all. He was in a cold, smelly, and crowded
cattle car.

"Awake, huh?" Pogue asked.

"Yeah," Cade answered, sitting up. "You want the space
to lie down?"

"No need. We'll be there in another half hour."

"How do you know?"

"We're in Chicago now," Pogue said. "If you look out the
left side of the car you'll see the city; if you look out the right
side, you'll see the ocean."

Cade chuckled. "It's not an ocean, it's a lake."

"The hell it is," Pogue said. "I ain't never seen me no
lake like this. Why, you can't even see the other side of it."

The train began slowing.

"We're there, boys!" someone called. "I can see a bunch
of blue bellies standin' out there a' waitin' for us."

A moment later the train came to a stop and shortly after
that, the door was jerked open.

"All right, out of the car!" someone shouted.

The prisoners jumped down from the car onto ground that
was covered with snow. It was very cold, and none of the
prisoners had coats. Cade was fortunate in that he, at least,
had shoes. Many did not.

"Form up, form up!" a Federal sergeant started yelling.

When the prisoners didn't get into a formation quickly enough to satisfy the sergeant, he stepped in and using a club, knocked a couple of them down.

"You men was in the army wasn't you? What the hell? Don't you Rebs know how to get in formation? Now form up, I ain't goin' to tell you again."

As the prisoners formed up in front of the cars, Cade had no idea what the temperature was, but he knew that this was about the coldest he had ever been in his life. He was standing in snow that was ankle deep, and he was chilled to the bone, wishing that he had a coat.

"All right, men, strip down!" the Yankee sergeant that was nearest to Cade and the men with him, shouted. Each of the prisoner formations had their own blue-clad sergeant in charge.

"Do what?" someone called out.

"Who said that?" the sergeant asked.

"I did," a prisoner in the second rank replied. "I want to know what you mean by strip down."

"Come up here, 'n we'll talk about it," the sergeant answered.

The prisoner complied, and as soon as he reached the front, the sergeant brought his club down, sharply, on the man's head. With a grunt, the prisoner fell to the ground.

"Now," the guard said to the others, standing over the prostrate form, slapping the palm of his left hand with the same club he had just used on the prisoner. "Let that be a lesson for you Secesh sons of bitches. I give the orders: you obey them. And no backtalk. I'll say it one more time, take off all your clothes and pile them on the ground in front of you."

If Cade had been cold, earlier, he was infinitely colder now.

After everyone was naked, the sergeant gave another order.

"All right, one at a time, pick up your clothes and bring 'em up to one of the guards who will be inspecting you for any hidden weapons you might have."

Cade saw, quickly, that the guards weren't just searching for weapons. They were confiscating any article of value, such as gold and silver watches, lockets, rings, pocket knives, and coins. Because Melinda's lock of hair was tied with a little strand of gold, Cade knew the guards would take it as well. How was he going to hide it? They would search his clothes, and he was totally naked.

Then he smiled. He had a perfect place to hide it. Unobserved, he took the lock from his pocket, then pushed it into his own disheveled hair.

"All right!" the sergeant called. "You Rebs get dressed now, and cover those shriveled up little peckers."

Cade put his clothes back on, but they had lain in the snow and were cold and wet so putting them on did nothing to make him any warmer.

The guard pointed to a high, blank, wooden wall that seemed to stretch forever. "In case you're wonderin', that there is goin' to be your new home. Onliest thing is, you ain't goin' to have your mama to tuck you in at night," he said with a smirk.

A guard stood near the gate, armed with a .54 caliber Springfield rifle. The gate was thrown open and Cade and the others marched through where they were assigned barracks. Cade and Pogue drew Barracks number 41, and once inside, they were given the first rations they had received since leaving the city of Nashville.

Lying in bed that first night, Cade assessed his situation. He was at Camp Douglas as a prisoner of war, with no idea how long he would be kept. He was also among strangers for the most part, he and Pogue Elliot being the only two men remaining from the twenty-man mess that had been together from the time the group was formed. Gordon Waters and Clint Copley had been killed. He knew that Jake, Timmy,

Harold, Abner, and Pete had also been killed. He didn't know about any of the others, and he didn't know what had happened to his brother. He and Adam were separated during the battle, then before he could find him, he was knocked down by a close blast.

When Cade had regained consciousness, he had no idea how long he had been out, but the battle was over; the sound of guns and screams were silent.

He jerked and groaned in reaction to a brutal kick in his side.

"Hey, Sarge, here's one that's still alive!" someone called out.

"How bad hurt is he?"

"How bad hurt are you, Reb?" the soldier asked.

"I, I don't know," Cade had answered, realizing then that the man was a Yankee.

"Can you stand?"

Moving some of the dead aside, Cade stood up, and though the effort made him a little dizzy, he didn't seem to be badly hurt. He was aware of blood running down his face.

"He can stand on his own!" the Yankee soldier called out.

"Send 'im over here. We'll put him with the rest of the prisoners."

As that memory faded, Cade took the lock of Melinda's hair then held it under his nose to breathe in her aroma.

Could he actually smell her? He didn't know if he could, or if he just thought that he could. But it didn't really matter, under the circumstances; perception was as good as reality. As long as he had her lock of hair he had her. Melinda was here, in this very cot with him. But it wasn't a cot, it was bed, their bed, in their own house, on their own farm.

Cade smiled, and kissed the lock of hair. As long as he knew he had Melinda waiting for him, he would get through this.

Each barracks had its own kitchen, the kitchen staff made up of prisoners. The kitchen was separated from the rest of the barracks by a partition. There was a window in the middle of the partition that was kept closed between meals. During the meal the window barrier would slide open, and the food, generally a weak broth with very little meat and fewer vegetables, would be pushed through the "crumb hole" as the prisoners called it.

Cade soon became friends with two more prisoners, Jed Carleton, and Albert Dolan. Cade already knew them, because both men had been in Captain Hanner's company, of the 33rd Tennessee; they just hadn't been in the same mess as Cade and Pogue.

At six feet two, Jed was an inch taller than Cade. Jed was a rather unusual man, who, because his father owned a riverboat company in Memphis, was wealthy enough to have bought himself a commission. He eschewed that opportunity though, choosing to serve as a private.

Before the war, Albert Dolan had been a deputy sheriff in Davidson County, Tennessee. He thought his experience should merit a commission and he complained, often, that a mistake had been made. He was somewhat resentful that Cade had been promoted to sergeant, and he hadn't.

"What difference does it make to us now?" Jed asked with a laugh. "We're all prisoners, and Cade doesn't have any more authority than any of the rest of us do."

"That's true," Cade said.

Dolan smiled. "Yeah, that's true, isn't it? How does it feel, Cade, to know that you aren't a sergeant anymore?"

"It feels great," Cade said. He put the back of his hand to his forehead. "The responsibility of command is just too much for me."

Dolan and the others laughed.

The four men: Cade, Pogue, Jed, and Dolan became inseparable, depending upon the friendship and mutual support to survive the ordeal that was facing them. Jed even gave the group a name.

"We are the Forty-one Quad," he said.

"What's that mean?" Pogue asked.

"We are in Barracks number forty-one, there are four of us. The Forty-one Quad."

"Yeah," Pogue said, understanding then. "Yeah, that's a good name for us."

The prisoners had been introduced to the various infractions that would draw punishment on the very day they arrived. Talking after six p.m., even quietly, would warrant punishment. So would cooking a meal on the stove, or even standing next to the single stove to get warm.

The most serious infraction was "gathering for a disturbance." Anytime a guard perceived that such a thing was happening, he was authorized to shoot to kill. Three prisoners, standing together in the prison yard, constituted gathering for a disturbance, and because of that, the Forty-one Quad could never be together when they were in the yard.

About a month after arrival, Cade, who had gone to get water without permission, learned first-hand the punishment called "riding the mule." The mule was a sixteen foot long saw horse, with a very narrow cross beam, elevated five feet off the ground. The prisoner being punished was forced to straddle this beam, the condition exacerbated by having as much as fifty pounds of weight tied to each ankle. That not only increased the pressure, the thin cords cut into the ankles.

The period of punishment was rarely less than two hours.

Albert Dolan and Jed Carleton were there to help Cade down from the device, and, because he couldn't walk on his own, one of them got on each side.

"Lean on us, we'll get you back," Dolan had said, sympathetically.

"Separate! Separate now or I will shoot!" a guard shouted.

"Go, Albert," Jed said. "I'm bigger than you are, I can handle Cade by myself."

A couple of days later, while on a work detail, Pogue managed to steal three loaves of bread from the guards' kitchen. That night, all the men of Barracks Forty - one gathered around to enjoy the unexpected bounty when the door to the barracks suddenly burst open and half a dozen guards came rushing in. The bread was confiscated and every occupant of the barracks was taken outside and forced to spend the rest of the night standing naked in the snow.

There were other incidents over the next several weeks where the guards seemed to have eyes in the back of their head, interrupting plans that the prisoners had made in total secrecy.

"I think we have a spy in our midst," Pogue said.

"What makes you think that?" Albert asked.

"Because it seems that no matter what we do, the Yankees find out about it. And I just don't think the Yankees are that smart."

"Why would someone spy?" Jed asked. "What would be in it for them? I mean you are suggesting it might be someone from the barracks, but if you look around, we are all in the same boat. Nobody seems to be getting any more food than anyone else, or any extra privileges. And when we spent the night outside, ever' one in the barracks was out there just as well."

"I don't know," Cade said. "Pogue might be right. It does seem like the guards know what we're going to do before we do it."

"If that's true, what do you suggest we do about it?" Albert asked.

"I don't think any plans we make from now on should go beyond the Quad."

"I agree," Pogue said.

"All right," Albert said. "I'm not convinced there is a spy in the barracks, but it won't hurt to be extra careful."

"That seems reasonable to me," Jed said. "From now on, we trust only the four of us."

6

SOON AFTER THAT DISCUSSION, the Quad undertook the most daring operation of all, plotting an escape while keeping the plans secret from everyone else in the barracks. Sneaking out at night when everyone else was asleep, they began digging a tunnel, starting under the barracks, and heading in the direction of the closest fence, which was forty feet away. They worked by twos, one man digging, and another standing watch. When they finished before morning, they covered the hole with boards, then scattered dirt over the boards so it couldn't be seen.

Three weeks after they started the tunnel, which was December 30th, 1864, they reached the other side of the fence.

"We'll go tomorrow, just before midnight, when the guards will be celebrating New Years," Cade said.

"After we get out, how are we going to get back home?" Pogue asked. "We're a long way from Tennessee."

"My father has a business associate here," Jed said. "I'll go see him. He'll lend us enough money to buy civilian clothes and the train tickets that will take us back."

"Won't he turn us in as escaped prisoners?" Cade asked.

Jed chuckled. "I know this man. Trust me, he is more loyal to business than he is to politics. And he'll want to do business with my father again, once the war is over."

"What do you want, Reb?"

"I want to talk to Colonel Sweet."

"What do you want to talk to the commandant about?"

"I want out of here."

"You think all you got to do is ask for a parole?"

"I've got something he's going to want to hear."

"You can tell me."

"No, I'll tell the colonel."

The guard stroked his chin. "All right, I'll take you to him. But this better be good, 'cause if it ain't, you're goin' to be sorry you ever brung it up."

"All right, prisoner, Sergeant Haverkost said you had something for me. What is it?"

"If the information is valuable enough for you, is it worth a parole?"

"It depends on what you have."

"Some men in barracks forty-one have been digging an escape tunnel."

"How far have they gotten?"

"They've finished it. It's ten feet beyond the fence at the northwest corner."

"You're sure about this?"

"Yes, sir, I know this for a fact."

"Well, that's farther than any of them have gotten in quite a while. When do they plan to make this attempt?"

"At midnight, tonight, when everyone is celebrating the New Year."

"Who are they?" Sergeant Haverkost asked. "I'll go get 'em 'n bring 'em to the colonel."

"No," Colonel Sweet replied with an evil sneer. "Let's let them think they are getting away with it. When they pop their heads up from the tunnel, we'll have a little surprise for them."

"Colonel . . . my parole?"

"Let's see if you are telling the truth. If some prisoners show up like you said, I think we can work something out."

On the night they were to leave, the quad waited in anticipation of the beginning of the celebration. By draw, Pogue would be first. Albert had drawn second, but he said he would rather go last.

"You want to see if the rest of us make it before you try, huh?" Jed teased.

"Yeah," Albert said. Of the four men, he was visibly the most nervous.

Jed moved up to second, and Cade third.

Outside the barracks they heard shouts and horns.

"Hey, Rebs! This is the year the South loses the war!" one of the guards called.

"All right," Cade said. "Pogue, you're first."

"Where's Albert?" Jed asked, looking around.

"I don't know, I thought he was right here," Cade said, noticing Dolan's absence.

"He must've got really scared," Pogue said. "Come on, we'll go without him."

Stepping out from the barracks, they crawled underneath then pulled the cover away from the opening to the tunnel. Pogue slipped down into it. Jed went behind him, and Cade was last.

Cade had a moment of indecision. He was supposed to pull the board back over the hole, but he decided to leave it open for Albert.

The men crawled quickly through the tunnel, then at the other end, which was beyond the fence, Pogue exited. Once he was out, he turned to help Jed.

After Jed was out, he reached back to offer a hand to Cade.

"Just where the hell do you Rebs think you're goin'?" a loud voice challenged.

"Get back! We've been caught!" Pogue shouted, just as the shots rang out. Pogue went down, and Cade, almost violently, jerked Jed back down into the hole. Crawling quickly the two men hurried back through the tunnel. When they exited the tunnel under the barracks, they collapsed the opening, then pushed over enough dirt to hide it.

When guards came into the barracks, fifteen minutes later, Cade and Jed were "asleep" in their cots. The guards walked down through the middle of the barracks, holding a lantern, checking everyone.

"All right, McCall, out of the bunk," one of the guards said. "You too, Carleton."

Both men were jerked out of their bunks.

"Are there any others, Sarge?" one of the other guards asked.

"Nah, Dolan said only three would be goin' out, 'n one of 'em won't be comin' back."

"Dolan?" Carleton said. "Dolan betrayed us?"

"He didn't betray nobody, Reb," Sergeant Haverkost said. "What he done was his patriotic duty."

"That's why he wouldn't come with us," Cade said.

"Don't worry Cade, Jed, we'll take care of the son of a bitch for you," a prisoner called out from the darkness, beyond the little golden bubble of light cast by the lantern one of the guards was carrying.

"You ain't takin' care of nobody," Sergeant Haverkost said. "Your boy, Albert Dolan is half-way to the railroad depot now. He'll be safe back in Tennessee, or Mississippi, or whatever the hell Secesh state he come from, before you two boys gets out of the hole."

The hole was an underground dungeon beneath the guard house. It was eighteen square feet and, at the moment, there were twelve men in it. It had a "sink" to handle the body waste and the smell was so strong as to be nauseating. There was no heat, and the extreme cold was barely tolerable due to the shared body heat from overcrowding. The only food was bread and water, and practically no one was able to eat because of the stench.

It wasn't that hard for most to go without food, because the conditions were so brutal, that the maximum punishment for offenses was usually three days.

Cade and Jed were given thirty days.

News of the unusually harsh punishment spread throughout Camp Douglas, and when new prisoners would come down, they couldn't help but feel compassion for the two men who had been in the hole so long.

"You two are heroes," one of the prisoners said. "The whole camp knows about you, 'n ever' one is prayin' for you."

"Yeah," one of the other prisoners said. "We figure that any of us who come down here can do three days easy, seein' as you all have so much time to do."

"Hey, Jed," Cade said, fifteen days into their confinement. "Growing up rich, like you did, I'll just bet you never thought you'd wind up sleeping in a bedroom like this, did you?"

"Ahh, a curtain here, a comforter there, it'll be just like home," Jed teased.

"Not that I'm glad you're in here, but, if I've got to be in this hell hole, I can't think of anyone I'd rather be in here with."

"Me too," Jed said. "I'm damn glad you're in here."

Cade reached up to run his hand through his hair, then he held it out toward Jed.

"Here's a couple of my pet lice, Alice and Jimmy. I'll let you play with them."

"Now I told you to keep those two separated. Next thing you know, we'll have a passel of baby lice to contend with," Jed said.

Both men laughed.

"You two are crazy!" one of the newest arrivals said. "Nobody can stand this place more than three days!"

"Oh, I don't know," Cade said. "Once you get used to it, it's not so bad. Especially since we get all the food you all won't eat."

"Like I said, you two are crazy!"

Cade and Jed laughed again.

After thirty days of such restricted confinement, Cade and Jed were let out. Neither of them were able to walk, and would have had to crawl back to Barracks forty-one if it hadn't been for some of the other prisoners who helped them.

The first thing each of them did was take a bath to get rid of the thirty days of filth. The water was barely above freezing, but they didn't care. At this moment the most important thing to them was to wash away the dirt, lice, and fleas. Getting clean again felt wonderful.

"Pogue was right," Jed said that night, when the two were able to stretch out for the first time in a month. "We did have a spy in our barracks. But who would have ever thought it would be one of the quad?"

June, 1865:

It had been six months since the failed escape attempt. During that time when things would get to the point of unbearable, Cade would take out the lock of Melinda's hair, and dream of the time they would be together again.

In that six months Cade's eyebrows had regrown, and the scar on his forehead, though still visible as a purple hook, was no longer puffy tissue.

Lee's surrender at Appomattox had been in April and though there had been rumors of their impending release, it had not yet happened. Then, on the morning of June twentieth, Jed came running into the barracks wearing a big smile.

"We're going home," he said. "They are setting us free, and giving us train tickets to wherever we want to go. Memphis, here I come!"

"I need to go to Nashville," Cade said. "From there, I'll take a boat to Melinda. I mean . . ."

"You don't have to tell me what you mean. Do you think I haven't seen you with that lock of hair? I tell you what. After you and your girl are married, come to Memphis to see me. As a wedding present, I'll arrange for you to go, first class, to New Orleans and back on one of Pop's finest paddle wheelers. How does that sound?"

"I don't care if we go in a rowboat, as long as I'm with Melinda."

Jed laughed. "I guarantee you, we can do better than a rowboat."

The Ladies Munificent League of Chicago had taken literally the Christian injunction to feed the hungry, and clothe the naked. After providing some of the released prisoners with a big meal, they made clothes available as well, replacing the rags their uniforms had become with clothes that were either new, or in very good condition. As a result, when Cade stepped off the boat in Clarksville, he, unlike many of the other returning war veterans was wearing civilian clothes.

Cade had thought to send his parents and Melinda a letter telling them that he was coming home, but he realized that he would be able to get here as quickly as any letter, so why not tell them in person?

The distance from Clarksville to the McCall farm was about four miles, and as Cade walked the route, he was soothed by the whisper of the Cumberland River alongside. A rabbit hopped up, ran quickly down the road before him, then darted back into the weeds.

"Hey, rabbit, why don't you run on ahead of me, and tell my folks I'm home?" Cade said aloud. "Think they'll be surprised? I wonder if I can talk Mom into making me a pot of chicken 'n dumplin's? Lord, it's been a long, long time since I've had chicken 'n dumplin's.

"I wonder which I thought about the most?" he asked, continuing his soliloquy. Though, as he was talking to the rabbit, he didn't look at it as talking to himself. "Did I think about Melinda the most? Or chicken and dumplin's?"

Cade pulled the lock of Melinda's hair from his pocket, and addressed it.

"All right, I'll admit it, I thought about you more than I did chicken 'n dumplin's but it was close. Real close. So close that maybe I'd better never even tell you," he finished, with a laugh.

The farm hadn't changed that much; the barn, the granary, and the smoke-house were still there. The windmill was a familiar sight. The house needed painting, there was very little about it to suggest that it had once been white. The steeply angled roof cut into much of the second story, and Cade could remember, fondly, reaching up from his bed to touch the wall which angled directly over his head.

Looking over toward a large magnolia tree he saw the little family burial plot. All four of his grandparents were buried there, as was Hazel, the sister Cade had never known. Hazel was the first born, but she died when she was two years old, six months before Cade was born.

But, wait a minute, there weren't five crosses in that plot. There were seven! Who were the other two markers for?

Moving quickly, Cade climbed the little hill, then stepped inside the low-level fence. The first cross he saw was for his father.

Jonathan McCall
Born in Kirkcaldy, Scotland August 5th, 1805
Died March 10, 1865

His father died in March? That was only three months ago. Cade felt an anger building up inside him. He was in a

Yankee prison when his father died, and because of that, he didn't even know about it.

The other cross was on the far side of the plot. He knew it wasn't his mother, if so, she would be lying next to his father. This cross was next to that of Hazel, so he knew it had to be for Adam.

"Adam, I'm sorry," he said aloud. "I should have kept you alive. It was my responsibility, and I failed."

Taking a deep breath, he stepped down to the other end of the little plot to examine the cross.

In Memory of
Cade McCall
Sergeant, 33rd Tennessee
Born 22 November 1843
Killed in Battle, 30 November, 1864

"What?" he said aloud. "What is this?"

"Cade? My God, is that you?"

Turning toward the voice, Cade saw Adam.

"I thought you were dead!" Both brothers said the same thing at the same time, then, hurrying toward each other, the brothers had a joyful embrace.

"What happened? Where have you been all this time?" Adam asked.

"I've been a prisoner of war in Camp Douglas," Cade said. "I wrote letters to Mom and Pop from prison. Are you saying they never received them?"

Adam shook his head. "No."

"Well, I can't say that I'm all that surprised. The way those Yankee bastards treated us, I'm surprised that anyone was ever able to get a letter through."

"I saw a cannon ball explode right beside you, and I saw you go down. The last time I saw you, you were lying in a pile of bodies, just outside the Yankee works. Then I went down with a minié ball in my leg, and wound up in a Yankee hospital in Nashville. I was paroled after that, but everyone said you were dead. Captain Hanner reported you dead, hell, you're even buried in the Confederate cemetery at Carnton Plantation. Or at least, someone is buried under your marker."

Cade smiled and put his hand on Adam's shoulder. "Well, little brother, as you can see I'm very much alive. I'm just going to go into the house now to see Mom, then I'm going over to the Waters' place and see Melinda. I can't wait to see her face when she finds out I'm not dead. Hey, you'll be the best man at our wedding!" Cade laughed out loud. "You have no idea how I have been hanging on to that thought."

"We thought you were dead," Adam said in a small voice.

Cade stepped back to the cross that bore his name, yanked it up, broke it across his knee, then tossed it aside. "Well, as you can see, I'm clearly not."

"Melinda and I both thought you were dead."

"Yeah, you keep saying that." Cade started toward the house. "I hope seein' me is not too big of a shock for mom. I'll have to . . ." Cade stopped when he saw a young woman standing on the porch. "Is that . . .?"

"It's Melinda," Adam said.

"Melinda? How did she know I was coming home?"

"We thought you were dead," Adam said again, more forcefully than before.

This time Cade listened, really listened, to what his brother was saying, and he realized that Adam was trying to tell him something, something that he didn't want to hear.

"Adam?" The eagerness and excitement in Cade's voice was gone, replaced by a plaintive tone.

"Melinda is my wife, Cade. We are going to have a baby."

If Adam had suddenly hit him in the stomach with a large club, it would not have been a more effective way of taking Cade's breath away. He stood there for a long moment, unable to move, unable to speak, barely able to breathe. His head was spinning so that he wasn't sure he would be able to stay on his feet.

"I'm sorry, Cade. We thought you were dead," Adam said again.

Cade's face showed both pain and rage, the expressions inseparable.

"We thought . . ."

"No!" Cade said, finding his voice. He held up his hand, and shook his head. "Don't say that again, please, for God's sake, don't say that again."

"All right," Adam said contritely.

Cade expelled a long breath. "I'll go see Mom," he said, once more starting toward the house.

"She isn't in the house," Adam said. "She's living in the cabin with Julius and Effie."

"What? Why on earth would she be staying in their cabin?"

"So Effie can take care of her. Cade, Mom's not well."

"Not well? What's wrong with her?"

"I think it's best if I let you see for yourself."

When Cade stepped up onto the small front porch of the little cabin a moment later, the black woman who opened the door gasped, and raised her hand to her mouth.

"Oh, Lawd a' mighty! Mr. Cade!" she said. "Is this real? You don't be a ghost, do you?"

"I'm not dead and I'm not a ghost," Cade replied. His reply may have been a bit sharper than he intended, but he was really getting tired of the constant expressions of surprise over him being alive.

"Oh, praise the Lawd!" Effie said.

"I'm told that my mother is here and that you are taking care of her."

"Yes, sir, yes, sir, she be here. Come in."

Effie stepped back and opened the door to invite Cade in. He saw his mother sitting at a table with both hands wrapped around a cup of coffee. He was a little surprised she was just sitting there, surely she had overheard the conversation he and Effie had. But then he realized that she might just be trying to get over the shock of learning that he was alive.

"Hi, Mom," he said. "Your prodigal son has returned," he added with a broad smile. Margaret McCall had always been a very religious woman and some of his earliest memories were of his mother reading the Bible. He thought she might appreciate the reference to the prodigal son.

Margaret showed no reaction to the reference, nor did she even look toward him.

"Mom?" Cade said, a little surprised by her lack of acknowledgement to his presence. He stepped up to her and put his hand on her shoulder. "Mom?" he said again.

Margaret looked at him, and, for the second time in the last few minutes, Cade felt the breath leave his body. There was nothing in her eyes.

"I like coffee," she said.

7

CADE WAS DRINKING a cup of coffee, liberally laced with whiskey. He was in the dining room, sitting across the table from Adam, whose own coffee was as strong as Cade's.

Melinda was in the living room, sitting on the sofa, knitting. She had not yet spoken to Cade, at least not in words. But her eyes and the expression on her face, said volumes. Cade knew, without having to hear the words spoken, that she was shocked by his return, and filled with the pain of what might have been, but now could never be.

"How long has Mom been like this?" Cade asked.

"She was like this when I got back, and Pop said she had been this way for over a year," Adam said. "It was Pop who moved her into the cabin with Effie and Julius, so Effie could take care of her."

"I don't think she even knew who I was," Cade said.

"She doesn't know me, she doesn't know Effie, she didn't even know Pop."

"What's wrong with her?"

"The doctor said it's called dementia. It just happens sometimes, he said, because when Pop was killed, she never even realized it."

"Yes, that's another thing. I saw on the marker that Pop didn't die until three months ago. He was killed, you say?"

"He fell from the loft in the barn, broke his neck when he hit the ground. He was dead by the time I got to him."

Cade nodded, then he looked toward the living room. "Melinda hasn't spoken to me."

"She's afraid," Adam said.

"Afraid? You mean she is afraid I would hit her or something?"

"No, we both know you better than that," Adam said. "She's afraid that she won't be able to explain what happened."

"Can you?"

"We thought . . ."

"Yeah, I know you thought I was dead. Take it from there."

"She was terribly distraught, Cade. Don't forget, Gordon was killed at Franklin, and she thought you were too. She lost a brother, and the man she loved. She was heartbroken, and she began spending a lot of time over here. I think, in the beginning, it was so she could feel closer to you. Pop and I were both devastated over you being killed, so having her here was sort of a comfort. We were comforting each other, really. Then, we finally got the courage to visit your grave at Carnton, or at least what we thought was your grave. And after that we . . . well, we fell in love. I'm sorry, but that's the way it happened."

Cade nodded, then leaving the dining room table, he walked into the living room where he stood, looking at Melinda. He didn't think he had ever seen anyone more beautiful than she was at that very moment.

"Melinda," he finally said. "Look at me."

She looked up from her knitting, and a tress of her long, blonde hair fell across one eye. She brushed it away, and Cade could see tears sliding down her cheeks.

"Oh, Cade," she said. "I am so sorry."

"It's all right, Melinda," Cade said. Subconsciously, he rubbed the purple, fish-hook shaped scar on his forehead. "I understand. I am hurt beyond words, but it was the circumstance that hurt me, not you. You and Adam are innocent and I love both of you. It's just that, now, I will love you as a sister-in-law."

When Cade and Adam returned to the house from a day of chopping cotton, they were met on the front porch by Melinda, who brought two glasses and a large pitcher of sweet tea.

"I cooled it as best I could by keeping it in the shade today," she said.

"I'm so thirsty, I could drink it if it was scalding hot," Cade said. "Thanks."

The two were drinking when Melinda held her hand over her eyes to look out onto the road.

"Someone's coming," she said.

Cade and Adam looked toward the visitor.

"Damn," Adam said. "It's Lloyd Botkins. What does he want?"

"Lloyd Botkins? Who is he?" Cade asked.

"He's a Yankee carpetbagger who came down here from Cleveland. Ever since he arrived, he's been buying people out. Hell, he owns more land now than anyone in Montgomery County."

"What does he want with us?"

"I don't have the slightest idea."

Lloyd Botkins was a short, rather rotund man, bald-headed except for a line of hair above each ear. He had a round face, full cheeks, an oversized nose, and rather small, beady eyes. He was wearing a cream - colored summer suit with a brown string tie. As soon as he stopped his one-horse shay, he wiped the sweat away from his face with the handkerchief he held.

"Good afternoon," he said.

"Mr. Botkins," Adam replied.

"My, that tea looks awfully good," he said.

"I'll get you a glass," Melinda replied and she stepped back into the house.

"What brings you out here, Mr. Botkins?"

"Oh, I thought you and I might talk a little business. That is, if this gentlemen would excuse us," he added, nodding toward Cade.

"This gentleman is my brother," Adam said. "And any business that has to do with me, has to do with him as well."

"All right," Botkins said.

At that moment Melinda returned with another glass, filled it with tea, and handed it to Adam, who stepped down to give the glass to Botkins.

"I thank you kindly, ma'am," Botkins said, lifting the glass then draining it all.

"The business, Mr. Botkins?" Adam said, retrieving the now empty glass.

"How many acres of cotton do you have in?"

"Forty acres. Why, have you added being a cotton broker to all your other business dealings?"

"Not exactly, but it does relate to the business we have to discuss. Right now, cotton is bringing about fifteen cents a pound. Now say you aren't hurt by a bad drought, then you should bring in about a bale an acre. That would be seventy-five dollars an acre, or $3,000 for the forty acres."

"I'd say that's about right," Adam said.

"I would like to propose that I buy your crop right now, forty bales, at fifty dollars a bale."

"Why would we do that?" Cade asked. "You just said yourself that cotton would be selling at seventy – five dollars a bale."

"Ah, yes, but you see, that is only if you make a good crop. Why who knows what could happen this year to prevent you from making a crop? You could have a drought, or it could go the other way, we could have rains so severe that the Cumberland overflows its banks and your entire farm could be flooded out. I'm not from here, but I understand that it has happened before."

Cade remembered a flood when he was fifteen, in which their entire crop was lost.

"Yeah," Cade said. "It has happened before."

"You could call my offer... insurance."

"No, thanks," Adam said.

"I'm sorry you feel that way," Botkins said. "Because you see, you have another thing to consider, an obligation you might say, to pay off your mortgage."

"Our mortgage isn't due until January, and then only one half of it. If we have even a normal cotton crop, we'll have enough money to make the payment," Adam said. "C.D. knows this."

"You would be talking about C.D. Lewis, of the First Bank of Clarksville?"

"Yes, who else would I be talking about?"

Botkins shook his head. "I'm afraid that Mr. Lewis no longer has anything to do with it," he said. "You see, Mr. McCall, I have bought the mortgage to your farm, and I have also paid off the taxes due. This farm is indebted to me for two thousand two hundred and eleven dollars. Now, if you would see fit to sell me your crop of cotton, today, for the price I have offered, you would only have to come up with another two hundred and eleven dollars."

"You don't really expect us to take that offer, do you, Botkins?" Cade asked. He left out the "Mister" because the man was beginning to irritate him. "The crop will make us three thousand, and like Adam said, we have until January to pay half of it."

"Oh, no, gentlemen, you don't understand," Botkins said. "As I said, I hold the mortgage now, and I am calling all of it in, in sixty days. That will be the end of August, which is before your cotton will make." He picked up the reins to his horse. "You might want to reconsider my offer to buy the cotton now."

Botkins made a clucking sound, snapped the reins, then pulled the shay around and started back.

"Oh, Adam, what are we going to do?" Melinda asked.

It didn't escape Cade's notice that Melinda asked Adam, and not him, what they were going to do. She thought of Adam first . . .any connection she may have once had with Cade was over. And who could blame her? It had been over three years since he first left, and three years was a lot of separation.

"I don't know," Adam said.

"Adam, how did we get in this position in the first place?" Cade asked. "I know that we owned this land outright, no mortgages of any kind. And I know that Pop was a very frugal man. How is it that we are now in debt?"

"Confederate money," Adam replied. "Like almost everyone else around here, Pop traded in his greenbacks for Confederate money. Seventy – five hundred dollars. The state didn't redeem the Confederate money, and neither did the Federal government. Everyone lost everything. Mr. Waters wound up losing his entire farm."

"Your father?" Cade asked, looking toward Melinda.

"Yes," Melinda said. "Papa and Mama are living in Nashville now. They have a single room at a boarding house, and Papa is working as a grocery clerk."

"Botkins owns the farm now. And the Byrd land that you and I once talked about buying? Botkins owns that too. This farm is the only farm Botkins doesn't own, between the Cunningham Pike, and the river."

Clarksville, TN:

Cade was waiting in The First Bank of Clarksville for a meeting with C.D. Lewis. He planned to ask for a loan, though he knew the chances of getting it were very small. After all it was Lewis who had sold their mortgage in the first place.

At the moment he was reading a newspaper, his attention drawn to one particular article.

Embrey R. Carleton, of Carleton River Transportation, has just put on two new boats for service between Memphis and New Orleans, Louisiana. Each boat is three hundred feet in length, and seventy-five feet wide.

"Each boat can carry 4500 bales of cotton," Jed Carleton has reported. Jed Carleton, who is Embrey Carleton's son, is vice president of Carleton River Transportation.

"You are the money courier?" Cade heard someone say.

"Yeah, Vernon Parker's the name."

"Here is your authorization to pick up the money, Mr. Parker. It is a bank draft, signed by Mr. Lloyd Botkins, and drawn against his own funds. Present this to Mr. David Jenkins at the First Bank of Nashville, and he will give you five thousand dollars in cash."

"All right."

"It is too late for you to get to Nashville before the bank closes today, but you must be there by the time it opens tomorrow morning, so you can be back here before close of business tomorrow afternoon. Mr. Botkins is very adamant about that. He wants the money here, tomorrow."

"You tell him not to worry," Parker said. "I've got a good fast horse, I'll be back in plenty of time."

Laying the paper aside, Cade walked to the front of the bank and watched as Parker mounted his horse, a big black, with a white face, and a large white circle on his right hindquarters. It was a distinctive enough horse to be recognized from some distance.

"Sir," someone said, stepping up to Cade then. "It looks as if Mr. Lewis isn't going to be back today. Perhaps tomorrow. If you would give me your name, I could make you an appointment."

"No, that's all right, tomorrow isn't convenient for me," Cade replied. "Perhaps I'll try and make an appointment next week."

"Very good, sir."

"I think I might have a solution to our problem," Cade told Adam when he got back to the farm.

"What would that be?"

"Do you remember Jed Carleton?"

"Carleton?"

"Yes, he was in our same company."

"Oh, yes, I do remember him. Wait a minute, he was that rich guy, wasn't he? Everyone used to talk about how he could have bought a commission, but he came in as a private."

"Yes. Jed and I were prisoners together in Camp Douglas, and we became very good friends. As a matter of fact, I saved his life once."

Cade was talking about when he jerked Jed back down into the escape tunnel just after the guards shot Pogue, and before they could shoot him.

Adam smiled. "Yes, I should think that would make you a very good friend."

"Jed told me once that if I ever needed anything, to come to Memphis and he'd help me out. Well, I need something, so I'm going to Memphis."

"You think you can borrow some money from him?"

"Yes, I do."

"How? We don't have enough equity in the farm, and if you borrow against the crop, as soon at the crop comes in and we pay him, we'll be back in the same boat again. We won't owe anything, but we won't have any money, either."

"That won't be your problem."

"What do you mean?"

"Adam, I can't stay here. You . . . Melinda . . . I can't . . . well, as I said, I don't hold that against you but it's just too distressing. The farm is yours, all yours. And the loan from Jed, that will be yours as well. You can call it my wedding present."

Adam shook his head. "No, Cade, I can't let you do that."

"Call it my payment for you looking out for Mom."

"When are you leaving?"

"Tonight."

"Do you want a horse?"

"What would I do with it? I'll be on a riverboat. A horse would just get in the way."

"But, how are you going to get to Memphis?"

"I'll take a boat tomorrow from Clarksville to Nashville, from there to Paducah, from there to Cairo, and from there to Memphis. I'll be there in about a week, and I'll send you the money so you can buy back the mortgage from Botkins, long before it is due." Cade smiled. "The only thing I regret is that I won't be able to see that son of a bitch's face when he is paid off."

"Yeah, I have to confess, I'm looking forward to that as well."

"Bye, brother," Cade said, sticking his hand out.

"Wait, let me get Melinda."

"No," Cade said, uttering the word more sharply than he intended. He held up his hand. "Please don't, Adam. I'd rather you not."

8

BEFORE LEAVING, Cade went out to the wood shed. Sticking his hand behind a piece of slab-wood nailed to the rafters, he smiled when he discovered it was still there. He pulled down a little canvas bundle and opening it, saw a Colt Revolver, leather holster, powder flask and several .44 caliber balls. Sticking the powder flask and lead balls into his pocket, he walked down to the river, then headed south.

Cade reached Half Pone Creek within three hours after he left, and spent the rest of the night there, using his rucksack as a pillow.

As Cade lay there, he stared up at the dark sky, filled with stars from those that were so bright he felt almost as if he could reach up and pluck one from the sky . . . to the ones that grew dimmer and dimmer until they became indistinct, other than a powder-blue dusting against the black velvet.

He thought about Melinda. Why hadn't she waited? Didn't she have any idea what she meant to him? Didn't she know that it was the thought . . . no, it was the sure and certain knowledge that they would be together for the rest of their lives that had sustained him? It had given him the courage to face death in a dozen battles, and the strength to survive the hell of a Yankee prison. But she had taken that courage and strength from him, and as he lay here, tonight, he felt as empty as a rag doll.

No. He wasn't being fair. It wasn't Melinda's fault. She thought he was dead, Adam thought he was dead, before he died, his father had thought he was dead, and the belief that he was dead might well have been the cause of his mother's dementia. It was time to put all that behind him.

"The rest of my life begins tonight . . .this very moment," Cade said aloud.

And as if to punctuate his statement, a meteor sped through the stars above him.

The next morning he pulled a little skillet and some bacon from his rucksack and had breakfast, though without coffee, as he had no way of making it.

It was about noon when he saw the courier coming up Ashville Pike, which was the road that ran between Nashville and Clarksville. It was easy to spot him, because of the distinctive markings of the horse. Cade was prepared for the encounter, he had already charged his pistol, and last night, before he left the farm, he had made a hood from an empty flour sack. He pulled the hood over his face and, with the pistol in hand, waited until the courier was near. When Cade stepped out into the road, his appearance was so unexpected that the rider's horse reared up, and had to be brought under control.

The rider, seeing an armed and masked man standing in front of him, started to reach for his gun. Cade fired his pistol, the bullet knocking the courier's hat off.

"I could a' put that right betwixt your eyes," Cade said. "Now, what I want you to do is pull that there pistol o' your'n, 'n drop it onto the road. But iffen I see anythin' more'n just your finger 'n thumb a' touchin' that gun, I'll shoot you dead."

Cade affected the most profound country accent he could.

The courier did as he was directed.

"Very good, Parker, maybe you ain't as dumb as you look. Now, I want you to come down from that horse."

"You know me?" Parker asked, surprised at being addressed by name.

"Hell yes, I know you. How could I ever forget a sumbitch like you?" Cade replied.

"Are you saying we're friends?" Parker asked.

"Oh I wouldn't say that me 'n you was ever exactly friends. We was a long way from bein' friends."

"Foster! That's who you are, ain't it! You're Fred Foster!"

"Parker, I done told you to get down offen that horse, 'n you got two ways o' doin' it. You can either climb down, or I'll shoot you down."

"I'm gettin' down, I'm gettin' down," Parker said, dismounting quickly. "Wait, you ain't Foster. I heard he was kilt in the war. You're Shoan, ain't you? Yeah, that's who you are. You're Abner Shoan."

"Stick your arms behind you, on each side o' this here tree," Cade said, continuing to exaggerate the affected dialect.

Parker did as he was told, and Cade secured him to the tree by using a strip of rawhide to tie his thumbs together.

The horse had stood patiently in the middle of the road and walking back to it, Cade picked up Parker's pistol, which was a later model Colt that utilized metallic cartridges, rather than the cap and ball Cade was carrying. He stuck the pistol down into the waist of his pants, then he opened the pouch, where he saw three packs of twenty dollar bills. Stuffing the bills down into his rucksack, he mounted the horse.

"Shoan! You'll never get away with this!" Parker shouted. "You hear me! I know who you are now, 'n I'll by God come after you myself!"

Cade rode off in the direction of Nashville, taking the hood off as soon as he rounded the first bend. About two miles before he reached the small town of Burns Station, he dismounted, then slapped the horse on the rump.

"Go home, boy," he said. "I won't be needing you anymore."

It wasn't by accident that Cade had chosen Burns Station. The Nashville and North West railroad ran through the town, and just as he reached the depot, he saw a freight making up. Cade waited until he was certain that there were no railroad workers who might see him, then he climbed through the open door into a freight car.

It was dark by the time the train started slowing down for Johnsonville. Cade jumped down from the train before it came to a stop, then walked the last quarter of mile into town. There had been a battle fought here between Nathan Bedford Forrest and the Federal forces who had occupied this town on the Tennessee River. The engagement was fought only a few weeks before the battle at Franklin, and though Cade had not been a part of it, he was well aware of it, for it had been a great victory for General Forrest.

Cade walked down to the water and saw that a riverboat was tied up at the dock. The boat, a side-wheeler, was a 'local trader', of the type that worked the Tennessee River. It was about half the size of the boats that plied the Ohio and Mississippi. A sign, on the front of the pilot house, identified the boat as the RUTH ANN.

While on the train, Cade had thrown both pistols away, and, except for a single, twenty dollar bill, he had rolled the three packets of bills up into his long handle underwear, and stuffed it down into his rucksack. Now, with the rucksack on his back, he walked down to the boat. There was someone on the main deck, leaning forward with his arms resting on the railing.

"Is the Captain aboard?" Cade asked.

"Yeah, he's aboard."

"Could I come speak with 'im?"

The man lifted his hand as if telling Cade to wait, then he left, and a moment later returned with another man.

"I'm Captain Hayes," the man said.

"Captain, I need to go to Paducah, and I was hoping I could work my way there."

The captain shook his head. "Sorry, I've got a full complement now, no need for another. I can take you on as a paying passenger."

"I don't have much money. What is the very cheapest fare you have?"

"You can buy deck passage for two dollars," Captain Hayes said. "That means that, rain or shine, you'll be on the deck for the two days it'll take us to get there."

"What about food?" Cade asked. "I wouldn't want to go two days without food."

"You'll eat with the deckhands," Captain Hayes said.

"That'll be fine."

"How'd you get that scar on your forehead?"

"I got it during the war."

Captain Hayes nodded. "Glad to hear you didn't get it in a fight. I don't want trouble on my boat. All right, come aboard. There are some sacks on the afterdeck. You can bed down on a couple of them for tonight, and settle with the purser tomorrow."

"Thank you."

At mid-morning the next day the boat was well underway, and Cade was leaning on the railing, just as he had seen the deckhand doing the night before. He was standing behind the starboard side wheel, and he could see the frothing water that was agitated by the beating of the paddles.

Reaching down into his pocket Cade pulled out the little lock of Melinda's hair, the same lock that had sustained him during the hellish days as a prisoner of war at Camp Douglas. He held the blond strands for just a moment, letting the bittersweet memories play through his mind, then he dropped it into the water. For a long second it rode atop one of the ripples of the paddle wake, extending the connection between

Cade and Melinda, then it was sucked down into the swirling eddies, and he didn't see it again.

In Paducah, Cade, as he had on the RUTH ANN, bought deck passage on the boat THE BUCKEYE. Just over a week after leaving the farm, Cade was in Memphis, in the office of Carleton River Transportation, standing before the desk of a rather small, bald-headed man wearing wire rim glasses which made his eyes look larger than they were.

No longer passing himself off as someone on the edge of abject depravation, he was now wearing new clothes, and carrying a leather satchel.

"Yes, sir, may I help you?" the greeter asked.

"I would like to speak with Jed Carleton."

"And may I tell Mr. Carleton who is asking for him?"

"Yes, my name is Cade McCall."

"Wait here, Mr. McCall," the man said.

A moment later Jed came rushing through the door toward Cade, moving even ahead of the greeter. He had a big smile on his face.

"Cade, you old son of a gun! Damn, I'm glad to see you!" he said, as he extended his hand.

"Hello, Jed," Cade replied, matching his friend's enthusiastic greeting.

"What brings you to Memphis?"

"I came to see you."

"Well, good! I want you to meet my father," Jed said. "I've told him all about you."

Embrey Carleton stood when Jed introduced Cade. Cade could see where Jed got his size, because Embrey was a big man, though age had caused flesh to replace the muscle he once had. Years had also turned his hair, and full beard white.

"Mr. McCall, may I tell you what a pleasure it is for me to meet the man who kept my son sane? How anyone survived that hell hole is beyond me."

"We leaned on one another," Cade replied.

"Then I'm glad you were there for each other," Embrey said.

"Mr. Carleton, I have a favor to ask of you."

"All right." The reply was somewhat nebulous, as if Embrey wasn't prepared to make a full commitment, without knowing the request.

"I have a rather large sum of money I would like to send back home, but of course, I don't want to send cash. Would it be possible for me to give you the money, and have you send a bank draft on your account to my brother?" Cade asked.

"I see no problem with that," Embrey replied.

Cade took out two bound packets of twenty dollars bills, counted out 175 of them, then passed them across the desk. Embrey picked them up.

"Who should I make this payable to?"

"Adam McCall."

"I'll have Mr. Reardon take care of this for us, it'll take a while," he said.

"Hey, Cade, what do you say you and I go eat while we're waiting on the draft?" Jed suggested. "I think we can beat the crumb hole."

"The crumb hole?" Embrey asked.

Both Cade and Jed laughed.

"It's a place where we used to go to eat," Jed said, without further explanation.

Half an hour later, the two men were at the River Café at the foot of Beale Street. It had been a while since Cade had really enjoyed a meal, and he stuffed himself with catfish, fried potatoes, hush puppies, sliced tomatoes, and dill pickles.

"Tell me, Cade, did you ever think we would actually be able to laugh about the crumb hole?" Jed asked.

"I never did, but I have to say that it feels good to laugh about it now."

"Listen, you didn't bring your two pet lice, Alice and Jimmy with you, did you?" Jed asked.

"You know, I was never able to get them house-broken, so I had to leave them behind.

"It's just as well."

They were quiet for a moment longer. "What brings you to Memphis by yourself?" Jed asked. "I thought, for sure, you would have Melinda with you. Remember, I promised you all a trip to New Orleans, first class, on one of our boats."

Cade was quiet for a long moment before he spoke. "They thought I was dead."

"What?"

"They thought I was dead," Cade repeated, and even as he was speaking the words, he realized that he was only mimicking his brother. "It turns out that I'm buried at Carnton Plantation. Or at least someone is buried there, under a marker that has my name. My father, Adam . . . Melinda . . . they all thought I was dead."

"Oh Lord," Jed said, understanding now. "Melinda married Adam, didn't she?"

"And now she's going to have his baby."

"That can't have been a very good homecoming for you."

"It was . . . uncomfortable. I had to leave."

There was another pregnant pause before Jed broke the silence. "The thirty-five hundred dollars?"

Cade looked up quickly. "What about it?" he asked, his voice almost a challenge.

"That's a lot of money. Where . . .."

"Let's just say I saw an opportunity, and I took it."

For the remainder of the meal the two spoke of shared experiences, not only in the prison, but during the time before.

"You remember Lieutenant Nox? How he always managed to be at the rear, 'hurrying up the stragglers?'" Jed asked with a laugh.

"And how Private Olsen use to call out, 'mama, mama, mama!' during a battle?" Cade added.

They shared other stories for the remainder of the meal, then they started back to the office, which was but one block south.

"Do you need any money, Cade?"

"No, I'm fine."

"All right, if I can't give you money, I'd like to offer you another opportunity."

"What is that?"

"It might be good for you to get away from Tennessee. I mean, given the situation with Melinda and your brother."

"That's probably a pretty good idea."

"We have a boat leaving for New Orleans tomorrow morning. When we go back to the office to pick up the bank draft, I'll arrange for first class passage for you on the MARY KATE."

Cade smiled. "Thanks, Jed. I'll just take you up on that."

The McCall Farm:

Melinda saw Julius Decker coming back from town, where he had gone for supplies, and to pick up the mail. She stepped outside just as he rode his mule, Rhoda, up to the porch.

"Hello, Mr. Decker," she said. "Were you able to get everything?"

"Yes'm I got it all," Julius replied. "'N I also got this letter which don' look nothin' like none of the letters you 'n Mr. Adams most of the time gets." He handed the envelope to her and, as he said, it was different in appearance. The envelope was pre-printed with the return address of Carleton River Transportation, 45 Gayoso Avenue, Memphis Tennessee. There was also a woodcut representation of a riverboat. It was addressed to Adam.

"Effie in the field, is she?" Julius asked.

"Yes, she's chopping cotton with Adam."

"I expect I'll go out there too, soon as I get these things put away," Julius said, taking down the burlap bag that was hanging from the saddle horn.

"Thank you, Mr. Decker."

Melinda thought about opening the envelope, then decided against it. It was, after all, addressed to Adam. She was going to wait until he came in, but curiosity got the best of her, so, with envelope in hand, she headed toward the south forty.

Adam looked up and smiled at her as she approached. He leaned on the hoe, then took out a handkerchief to wipe the sweat from his face.

"Hello," he said.

"Julius picked this up from the post office," Melinda said, handing the envelope to Adam.

"What is it?"

"I don't know, it's addressed to you, and I'm too curious to wait to see what it is."

"All right," Adam said. "We'll see together."

Adam removed the contents from the envelope, read them, then pulled everything to his chest and looked at Melinda with a shocked expression on his face.

"My God," Adam said.

"Adam, what is it? You are frightening me!"

Adam handed the papers over to Melinda.

"Look at this," he said. "Look, Melinda!"

Dear Adam,

You probably won't hear from me for a while, I feel the need to travel for a bit. Here is bank draft for $3,500. I got very generous terms for the loan, which I will be able to handle myself, so there is no need for you to pay it back. This is my wedding gift for you and Melinda.

Sincerely, Your brother
Cade

9

CADE COULD NOT IMAGINE any contrast more extreme than his arrival in Memphis as a deck passenger on a cargo boat, and his departure from Memphis as an occupant of first class quarters on the MARY KATE. The most dominating feature of the room was a big, brass-frame bed, though the room was so large that it wasn't overpowered by that piece of furniture. In addition to the bed, there was a sofa, a dresser, and a chifferobe.

Part of the enjoyment was the marvelous meals that were served. For the first time in his life, he ate loin of lamb, with mint sauce.

The next morning he walked out onto the forward section of the hurricane deck just before sunrise. At this hour, there was nobody else on deck, and he felt a haunting sense of loneliness, isolation, and remoteness from the rest of the world. Except for the breeze created by the boat's passage, there was not the faintest breath of wind.

He could hear a solitary bird, singing to the morning. Other birds joined in, and soon the pipings developed into a jubilant riot of music. As the day grew brighter, Cade enjoyed the intense green of the foliage that crowded down from each side of the river. Then, with the sun well up, the river came alive as a path of shimmering gold.

Cade looked at the river as it lay before him.

"I wonder," he said speaking aloud, confident that no one would be able to hear him, "if I could travel fast enough, far enough, could I look into the future and see what lies ahead?"

He shook his head. "No," he said. "Nor would I want to."

He thought back to his time during the war, and in the Camp Douglas prison. He was convinced that it was thoughts of Melinda that had gotten him through that ordeal. What if he had known then, what he knew now, that she wouldn't be there? It would have been infinitely harder for him.

"It was certainly a pleasure having you aboard, Mr. McCall," the captain said as Cade left the boat in New Orleans late in the afternoon of the day they arrived. "I hope your trip was a pleasant one."

"It has been a most enjoyable experience, Captain. I can't think of a thing that would have made it better."

Leaving the boat, Cade walked up Decatur Street, which ran parallel to the river basin, where he saw a forest of masts, free of sail. As he passed each of the ships, he read the names: HARRIET LANE, BAYOU CITY, WESTFIELD, ROB ROY, FREMAD, and the DART.

The display of so many ocean-going ships was interesting, because he had never seen such a thing before. But he was more interested in exploring New Orleans. He had fourteen hundred and twenty-seven dollars in the satchel he was carrying, and forty-three dollars in his pocket, which, he was certain, would be enough to enjoy himself.

New Orleans assailed every sense. He heard a cacophony of sound from the clip-clop of the horse's hooves striking the stone paving blocks, music emanating from the bars; pianos mostly, but from at least one, the mellow wail of a saxophone. He heard, also, a mixture of languages being spoken, with English and French predominating.

New Orleans was a visual treat as well, with grand public buildings alongside elegant manors and narrow townhouses. The most noticeable structures were the two story buildings with hipped roofs and expansive balconies, enclosed by wrought-iron railings.

Cade started to walk by a building that bore a sign identifying it as Tujague's. The name meant nothing to him, but the smell coming from within made his stomach rumble in anticipation. It was nearly suppertime, and Tujague's was obviously a restaurant.

Realizing that he was hungry, and intrigued by the unfamiliar, but enticing aromas, he stepped inside. The restaurant was filled with what appeared to be workingmen; merchants, laborers, as well as sailors and boatmen from the docks. After he was seated, he was approached by a waiter.

"Today we are serving shrimp remolade, crawfish etouffee, boiled beef brisket, or andouille with red beans and rice."

"You are serving all that? I'm hungry, but I don't think I could eat that much."

"You don't get them all, you choose one of the four."

"The only two things I recognize are beef, beans and rice. I've eaten beef, but I've never eaten shrimp. I think I would like to try that."

"All right."

In no time at all, it seemed, the waiter returned with a plate, which he set in front of Cade. He had never actually seen shrimp before, and his first impression of them was that they looked like large bugs. He stared at them for a moment, unsure as to what to do.

"Dip them into the remolade," the waiter suggested.

"The what?"

The waiter pointed to a cup that was filled with a thick sauce, mostly white, but liberally dotted with seasoning.

Cade picked up one of the shrimp and holding it by the tail, started to dip it into the sauce.

"You must remove the shell first," the waiter explained.

Cade nodded, peeled the shrimp, dipped it, then, hesitantly took a bite. Immediately, his mouth was assailed by a very spicy flavor. It was good, and he smiled broadly as, continuing to chew, he looked up at the waiter.

"BON APPETIT," the waiter said as he withdrew.

After leaving the restaurant, Cade continued his exploration of the city, and on the corner of St. Phillip and Bourbon Street he saw a relatively small brick building with a steep shingled roof and dormers. The sign read "Lafitte's Blacksmith Shop Bar."

Curious about the strange name, he stepped inside and saw that it was, indeed a bar. Virtually all the bar's clientele were sailing men.

"BIENVENUE MONSIEUR," a very attractive, petite young woman with dark hair and flashing black eyes greeted him. "MON NOM EST CHANTAL." When she saw that he didn't understand, she repeated it in English. "Welcome, Monsieur. My name is Chantal."

"Hmm, I don't think I've ever known a Chantal," Cade said.

"Then that makes me feel very special," Chantal replied with a broad smile.

"This doesn't look much like a blacksmith shop," he said.

"It began as such, under the hero, Jean Lafitte."

"Hero? The only thing I have read about him is that he was a pirate."

"OUI, but he also saved New Orleans from the British."

"I thought Andrew Jackson did that."

"They did it together. Would you like a table, Monsieur?"

"Yes, thank you."

"Come, I will find one for you," she offered.

There was something about Chantal that Cade found very arousing. He knew that was by design, after all, she was dressed to be provocative. In addition to her appearance, there was a scent about her, a sweet-smelling floral base perfume, enhanced by a note of her own femininity.

As he followed Chantal through the shadows of the bar, he began to feel a sense of excitement. Cade had never slept with a woman. He was too young before his relationship with Melinda got serious, he didn't want to cheat on her, and the opportunity had never presented itself since. But any idea of "saving himself" for Melinda was no longer a consideration.

"The son of a bitch should be keel hauled, if you ask me," a man at one of the tables said, speaking loudly enough for Cade to hear.

"They don't keel haul people anymore, Jimmy," another said. "I think there's a law or somethin' ag'in it."

"Yeah, I know, but back in my day, by God, if we had run across someone like Barkley, we would 'a keel hauled him in a minute."

"Carl Barkley is the second mate. Second mates aren't keel hauled."

"Then the son of a bitch should 'a been tossed overboard," Jimmy said. "I'll tell you this. As long as that bastard is second mate on the FREMAD, I'd sail on a garbage scow before I'd set foot on her deck again."

The conversation penetrated Cade's awareness only because he passed close by the table.

"You may sit here, Monsieur. I will get your beer."

"Thank you."

It appeared that animated discussions were taking place all over the room, but the table Chantal had selected was too far from the others for him to follow any of the conversations.

Cade set the satchel on the floor between his feet and waited until the woman returned.

"Here is your beer, Monsieur."

"Why do you keep calling me Monsieur?"

"Because I don't know your name."

"My name is Cade. Tell me, Chantal, why did you put me so far away from everyone? I'm lonesome over here."

"Oh, but you won't be lonely, Monsieur Cade. I'll be with you," Chantal said, as she coquettishly lowered her head and looked at him through half shaded eyes. "You do want my company, do you not?"

"Of course I do," Cade replied.

The woman smiled, then leaned forward, her movement displaying the mounds of her full breasts almost to the nipples.

"I think you like Chantal, OUI?"

"OUI, I like Chantal."

"There is a room upstairs we can use," Chantal said. "But I am not cheap."

Cade was light headed, and in addition to his obvious physical arousal, he felt his stomach rising to his throat.

"How much?" he asked, his voice so husky he almost didn't recognize it.

"Five dollars."

Ordinarily, five dollars would be an exorbitant amount of money. But he had much more than five dollars, and he didn't want to pass up the opportunity to be with a woman. And Chantal was not just any woman; she was an exceptionally beautiful, and sexually arousing woman.

"Let's go," he said, standing so quickly that he almost knocked the chair over.

For just a second, Chantal's eyes reflected some surprise over him acquiescing so easily to the price she had quoted. But the surprise was quickly replaced with her sensual invitation to an erotic interlude, "Oh my, has it been a long time, honey?"

"You have no idea."

Half an hour later, Chantal stood naked, her skin shining gold in the candlelight. Cade lay in bed with his hands laced behind his head, watching the beautiful creature as she was getting dressed.

"You must get up and get dressed, Monsieur Cade," Chantal said. "There are other girls who use this room as well."

"I will," Cade said. "I just want to watch you for a moment longer."

Chantal smiled, then as she moved, she stubbed her foot on something. "Oh, what is this?" she asked picking up Cade's satchel.

"Here, I'll take that!" Cade said, getting up quickly to reach for it.

"My, you seem most anxious. What have you got in here, Monsieur?"

"Nothing," Cade said, snatching it quickly. "Just some clothes."

"They must be very nice for you to be so concerned."

"There is nothing special about them. I just don't want to take a chance on losing them, is all."

Cade reached for his clothes, and because he could dress more quickly than Chantal, he was ready to go before she was.

"Monsieur Cade," Chantal said, in a soft and sultry voice. "You are so sweet, and so . . . manly," she added, suggestively. "If you will come see me again tomorrow, for just a few dollars more I will make the arrangements so we can have the room all night. You would like that, no?"

"I would like that yes!" Cade replied, enthusiastically.

He checked into a hotel on the corner of St. Louis and Chartres streets. As he lay in bed that night he considered the possibility of living in New Orleans. For more reasons than one, he needed to be away from Tennessee, and New Orleans seemed the perfect solution. Chantal was an additional incentive to that idea.

He knew what she was, and there was obviously no thought of a romantic attachment. On the other hand, why couldn't he maintain a friendship with her? It would be nice to know that there would always be someone there for him when he felt the need for a relationship that had neither restrictions nor boundaries.

To stay in New Orleans, however, he would need a job. He had enough money to support himself for some time, but he didn't want to depend on it, and he didn't want anyone to know that he had it. Tomorrow, he would look for work.

It was mid-afternoon of the next day, and Cade had practically exhausted all his options for finding a job. He had very little to offer any employer; he was experienced in only two fields: farming, and the army. He had left both the farm and the army behind him, and had no wish to revisit either occupation.

During the day he had applied for work in half a dozen bars, at a freight office, as an apprentice blacksmith, even as a policeman. His military experience might have gotten him on as a policeman, but there were no openings there.

Then he happened to pass the cotton exchange. Why not try here? He certainly knew cotton.

"What do you look for, in appraising cotton?" his job interviewer had asked him.

"Color, fiber length, uniformity, fiber firmness, and fiber strength," Cade replied.

The interviewer smiled and nodded. "Mr. McCall, come in Monday. You have a job."

10

"YOU ARE SURE he will come tonight?"

"Oui, Monsieur Lundy, he will come tonight."

"What is he like? Is he strong enough?"

"Qui. He is young and, very strong."

"What does he look like?" Lundy asked. "How will I recognize him?"

"He is a very handsome man."

"Handsome? How the hell am I supposed to know what a handsome man looks like? You need to give me more than that."

"He has auburn hair," Chantal said. "Oh, and there is a scar here, a purple scar, shaped so." With her finger, she traced a hook above her right eye.

"All right, I'll wait here until he comes in tonight."

"I will get my twenty dollars then?" Chantal asked.

"After I am paid," Lundy replied.

When Cade walked into the bar that evening there was an extra spring in his step. He had a job; there was no reason he would have to leave New Orleans.

"Monsieur Cade, you did come back!" Chantal said, greeting him happily.

"I told you I would."

"Do you want to go to the room right away?"

"Yeah, but I'd like a drink first. I've got some good news to tell you."

"Good news?"

"Yes, I have a job, Chantal. I'm going to stay in New Orleans. That means I'll be able to visit you anytime I want."

"Oh, Cade I . . ."

"Oh, don't get me wrong, I know how it is going to be. I know that I'm going to have to pay for the visits, but don't you see, I'll have a job, which means I'll be here. And I'll have the money to afford the visits."

"That is great news," Chantal said. "The news is so good that I think we should celebrate not here, but in the room with a whole bottle of Champagne."

"Champagne? I've never tasted champagne before."

"You will like it," Chantal promised.

Chantal walked over to the bar, spoke to the bartender, then returned to the table holding a green bottle.

"Come," she said, leading him toward the steps that climbed to the second floor. They went into the same room they had used the night before.

"And we don't have to leave?" Cade asked.

"I have it for as long as I want it," Chantal replied. She poured the champagne into two glasses, handed one glass to Cade, took the other and held it out.

Cade touched his glass to hers, and they both drank. There was a sparking sensation in his mouth, which, while strange wasn't unpleasant. They followed the first glass with a second, and then a third.

Very soon after he started drinking the third glass, Cade felt a lightness in his head, a lightness that seemed to suffuse his arms and legs, all the way out to his fingers and toes.

"What?" he said. "What's happening to me?" Cade asked the question very slowly, barely able to enunciate the words.

"Go to sleep now," Chantal said, smiling at him.

Cade stared down into his glass but saw nothing but the final few swallows of his drink. "I . . ." he started, but whatever he had in mind to say went unstated.

The world went black.

Chantal put her hand on his neck to feel for his pulse. She was glad to see the pulse was strong. She was never sure how someone would react to the chloral hydrate in the knock out drops. There was always the chance that the dose could be fatal, and though no one she had ever used the drops on had died, she had heard stories of just such a thing happening.

She started toward the door to notify Lundy, but as she did she saw the small, brown leather satchel that he always carried. Opening it, she looked inside and saw that it contained, as he had told her, clothes. She was about to toss it aside when she saw a twenty dollar bill. With a smile she reached for it and when she did, she felt two more. Then she grew curious and dumped all the contents out onto the bed. There, with the clothes, she saw more money than she had ever seen in her life.

"Mon Dieu!"

Half an hour later Lundy drove a buckboard down to the docks, where he was met by a big bull of a man with broad shoulders and strong arms. He had a sloping forehead, prominent eyebrow ridge, deep, dark eyes that darted about, a pug nose, and a lower lip that protruded from his mouth.

"How many do you have?" the big man asked.

"Three."

"Any of 'em sailors?"

"One is, for sure. He's Portuguese, a fella by the name of Bento Hernandez. He come in a couple of weeks ago on a French ship, the AIGLE DE MER."

"Yeah, I know that ship," the big man said. "What about the other two?"

"They've got strong backs, what else do you need?"

"You're right, I don't need anything else. All right, hold on for a bit until I can get someone to help me bring 'em aboard, then I'll pay you."

Awareness came to Cade, slowly. He was lying down, not on the ground, nor the floor, nor even a bed. He seemed to be lying on a suspended stretch of canvas. The room was moving, first going up where it seemed to hang suspended for a long moment, then a precipitous drop, the bottom of the drop augmented by a roll to the left and the right.

He was having trouble breathing, then he realized that the room was filled with smoke. At first he thought he might be in a building that was on fire, but then he heard some loud laughter, and realized that it was tobacco smoke.

He opened his eyes and saw that he was in a dimly lit place, uncomfortably close with the tobacco smoke, and filled with men, all of whom seemed to be dressed like the sailors he had seen at the bar.

He could hear the creak and strain of wood, and thought, though he wasn't sure, that he could hear the sound of water rushing by, just on the other side of the wooden wall he was lying against.

"Stumpy, you lucky son of a bitch! How did you draw that ace? I know damn well I put it way down in the deck just so's you couldn't draw it," someone said, and the little room was filled with laughter.

Cade sat up, and almost fell out, first because the strip of canvas he was lying on wasn't anchored, and also because his head was spinning. He felt a very bad taste in his mouth, and his head hurt.

"Where the hell am I?" he asked.

"The last one is awake," someone said.

One of the men walked over to him. "You've been out a long, long time. They must've given you one hell of dose," he said.

"Dose of what?"

"Whatever it is they give the fellas that get shanghaied."

"Shanghaied?"

"Yeah, we was about to sail with a short crew, but you 'n two others was brung aboard."

By now Cade was fully conscious and aware of his surroundings. He saw a lighted lantern hanging from the overhead, swinging back and forth in conjunction with a most definite roll. He was not only on board a ship, the ship was at sea.

"I'll be damn!" he said. "I'm on a ship!"

"That ye be, mate, that ye be," the sailor who had come over to speak to him said. The sailor had gray hair and beard, and was obviously older than all the others . . . some of whom couldn't have been more than seventeen or eighteen years old. "You're on board the FREMAD."

Cade remembered seeing the FREMAD when he left the MARY KATE. He also seemed to remember this being the ship that was being talked about by the sailors in the bar.

"The name is Burke, Josiah Burke. But most just call me Pops. What's your name?"

"Mc . . ." Cade started to give his real name, then thought better of it. "Copley," he said. "Pogue Copley." He didn't want to give his real name, and he thought that by combining the names of two of his friends, both of whom were now dead, he would be able to remember his alias more easily.

"It's good to know how to call you. When the contractor brought you three aboard, he didn't bother giving us any names."

"Who is this contractor?"

"He is the one who shanghaied us," another sailor said, speaking with an accent. This man was short and wiry, with a face that could best be described as weathered. It was really rather difficult for Cade to determine how old he might be.

"So, you are one of the three Pops is talking about? You came on board at the same time I did?"

"SIM. Yes. My name is Bento Hernandez."

"Are you Spanish?"

The wiry man made a spitting motion to denote his displeasure at the suggestion. "NAO. I hate the Spanish. I am Portuguese."

Cade looked at Pops. "You said there were three of us who were shanghaied. Who is the third?"

"Nobody knows, he ain't give us his name," Pops said.

"He ain't said nothin' a' tall," another put in. "He ain't done nothin' but lie there in his fart sack, cryin'." Smiling, he extended his hand toward Cade. "The name is Stumpy. Stumpy Jones."

"Hey, Copley, what's the last thing you remember?" Pops asked.

Cade started to say being in a room with a woman, but he altered his response. "Having a drink in a bar with a very pretty woman."

"Uh, huh. And do you remember the name of the bar?"

"Yeah, it was the Lafitte Blacksmith Bar."

Pops nodded. "Aye, that's a seaman's bar. Most of the time when they snatch somebody up, they take 'em from a seaman's bar."

"But that's kidnapping," Cade said. "You can't just grab someone and force them to so something against their will. How's that any different from slavery?"

"Slaves didn't get paid," Pops said. "You'll be makin' fifteen dollars a month, but you won't get none of it 'till the ship gets back. Sometimes that works out good though, 'cause once you're back on the beach, you can wind up with as much as a hunnert 'n fifty, maybe even two hunnert dollars to spend."

"Yeah," Stumpy added with a chuckle. "That's how come there's so many drunken sailors. They been at sea for a long time, 'n when they come back they got money and a big thirst."

"More often than not, by the time they've drunk up all their money, they're ready to come back to sea," Pops said. "'N a lot of them's that ain't ready, come back anyway, just the way you 'n Hernandez and the other fella done. You get shanghaied."

"Most sailors more or less expect it," Stumpy said. "Hell, if they didn't want to come back to sea, they wouldn't hang out in any of the port bars."

"You two talk like this is a normal way of doing business," Cade said.

"Yeah, you might say that it is," Pops said. "I've been shanghaied a couple of times myself."

"Listen, you bein' new 'n all, I figure maybe we should tell you about Barkley," Stumpy said.

"Barkley?" Cade asked. "The second mate?"

"Yeah, do you know 'im?"

"No, but I seem to recall hearing his name mentioned by some sailors that were in the bar, and I gathered they weren't particularly fond of him."

"Hell, his own mama couldn't be fond o' the son of a bitch," Stumpy said. "Anyhow, like I was sayin', you need to watch out for 'im. If he says shit, you don't ask how much, you just squat 'n do it. He loves to use a rope's end to make a point, but that's when he's goin' easy on you. What the son of bitch really likes to do is tie you to the mast so Higgins, the bo'sun can give you a real beatin'."

"Thanks, I'll keep that in mind. By the way, what is this place we're in now?" He took in the area with a wave of his hand. "What do you call this part of the ship?"

"This is the fo'c'sle," Stumpy said. "This is the crew's quarters."

"Foc's'le," Cade repeated. He ran his hand across the canvas that was his bunk, then hopped down and began looking around.

"What are you lookin' for?" Pops asked.

"When I was brought here, you didn't happen to see a brown leather satchel with me, did you?"

"No, I didn't see one," Pops said.

"They didn't none of you have nothin' with you," Stumpy said.

"Why you worryin' 'bout the satchel? Was they somethin' important in it?" Pops asked.

Cade started to tell them about the money, then decided not to. When he stopped to consider it, it wasn't really his money in the first place. And before he lost it, he was able to get a bank draft sent back to his brother, to save the farm, and that was the most important thing.

"No, the only thing I had in it was a change of clothes."

"Well then, that ain't nothin' to worry 'bout, 'cause them clothes wouldn't 'a done you no good no how," Pops said. "You'll have to wear sailin' duds long as you're on the ship."

"Where do I get those?"

"Cap'n Mumford keeps a slop chest," Pops explained. "You can outfit yourself from that, 'n pay 'im from your wages, once you collect."

"On deck!" someone shouted from the head of the companion ladder. "All hands on deck for the cap'n's words, and the pickin' o' the watch."

"You feel well enough to climb the ladder?" Pops asked.

"Yes, I think so."

"I'll climb up behind you to catch you in case you fall."

When they reached the deck Cade saw the open water of the Gulf itself.

"There goes the tug back to New Orleans," Stumpy said, pointing to a short, blunt-looking screw-propelled boat that was beating its way back. Looking in the direction the tug was going, Cade could see the land, and the wide mouth of the Mississippi, where it flowed into the Gulf. For just a moment he almost shouted out that he should be on that boat, that he had no business being on board the FREMAD. He even gave a passing thought to leaping overboard and trying to swim to it, but he knew that would be a foolish, and most likely, fatal gesture.

"Lay aft to the poop and stand respectful for the cap'n's words," a large man said. He was carrying a short piece of rope.

"That's Carl Barkley, our second mate," Pops said.

"Wait, wait! Signal that boat!" someone shouted. "Stop it immediately! I'm not supposed to be on this ship! I was kidnapped!" This was the third man who had been brought aboard with Cade and Hernandez.

"Quiet your bellowin', you whiney bastard!" Barkley said, and he augmented his commands with the generous use of the rope's end. "Now lay aft like I told you! All of you, lay aft, now!"

Barkley lashed out at a couple other sailors, whose only infraction was to be close enough for him to get to them.

Long Road to Abilene

11

CADE FOLLOWED POPS, Stumpy, Hernandez and the others aft, to the poop deck. Even though Hernandez, like Cade, had been shanghaied, he was an experienced seaman and had already accommodated himself to the situation, blending in with the rest of the crew as if he had been a willing recruit.

"You were kidnapped just as I was, weren't you?" the third of the three shanghaied said to Cade. He was young, Cade supposed in his late teens. He was blond, with blue eyes, and an innocent face, which suggested that he had experienced very little stress in his life before now. He was wearing black pants with a white, ruffled shirt.

"Yes, I was shanghaied," Cade replied.

"Why didn't you speak out when that villainous man beat me with the rope?"

"What good would it have done for me to have said anything? He wouldn't have stopped beating you, and I would have been next."

"I heard you tell the others that your name is Copley. My name Tait, Willoughby Tait. I think we should stick together. The three of us were illegally taken, and brought out here for a period of involuntary servitude. If we would unite in our petition to the proper authorities, I'm sure we would prevail."

"And just who do you think would be the proper authorities?" Cade asked.

"Why, those in charge of this ship, of course. I think that you, Mr. Hernandez, and I, should make a vehement protest. Now would be our opportunity, since the captain is about to make his appearance."

"Tait, you talk just real pretty, usin' them big words 'n all. But if you don't keep your mouth shut, you'll be getting' a lot more than a rope's end laid across your back," Pops warned. "Ye'd best be hushin' up now."

"Who are you to tell me . . ." Tait started to say, but Cade interrupted him.

"I'd listen to him if I were you. You said we should stick together? Seems to me like our best bet is to learn from those who know what they're doing."

A man, wearing a blue jacket with brass buttons, walked out on the poop overhang. Cade didn't have to be told that this was Captain Mumford. It was obvious, not only by his mode of dress, but by his bearing, which was that of a man comfortable with command. There were two men standing with the captain, one on either side. The man to his left was Carl Barkley. The other, Pops identified as Emerson Drake, the first mate. "Folks say that Francis Drake was a great, great grandpa or something like that, only I don't know whether or not that's true."

"Who was Francis Drake?"

"Why, ever' sailin' man knows who he was," Pops answered. "He's just about the most famous sea cap'n there ever was. Anyhow the first mate ain't so bad, whether he's actual akin to Francis Drake or not. He's satisfied with where he is. It's Barkley that's the real bastard. He has ambition, and there ain't nothin' worse than an evil man with ambition."

"Stand to for the Cap'n's words," First Mate Drake said, calling to a halt the mumbled conversation of the sailors there gathered.

Captain Mumford was standing on the edge of his domain, the poop deck, onto which no ordinary seaman, save the helmsman, could come unless specifically invited.

The captain was of average height and body conformation, but with a face that was weathered by many years at sea. Clearing his throat, he put his hands behind him and began to speak in a voice that was loud enough to be heard clearly by every man on the ship.

"Now, you men listen to me. Be reliable hands, and be aware of what's around you, and we'll do fine. Any man who turns into a malingerer will answer to Mr. Barkley, and he won't be gentle in dealing with you."

Captain Mumford nodded toward Barkley. The second mate was glaring at the men as if he could barely restrain himself from grabbing someone and throwing him overboard.

The captain continued. "I want no complaints from any of you. Most of you have been to sea before, and you know what is expected. You greenies, you'll soon learn that you aren't in your mama's house. There'll be no apple pie and sweet milk for you here, just salt meat and hardtack, a sailor's food. If you don't know your way about, find an old sailor to team up with, and do everything he tells you to do.

"Now," Captain Mumford went on. "Some of you may know that the FREMAD is bound around the Horn for San Francisco, with a hard stop at The Plate. It'll be difficult sailin' around the Horn, but I expect each man to stand his watch without complaining. Any man who doesn't will be tied to the mast and given enough lashes to correct the situation. Remember, each and every one of you belongs to me, body and soul. Now, stand by while the first and second mates pick the watches."

Drake, the first mate, had the first choice. "Miller!" he called.

"Burke!" Barkley followed.

For the next few minutes, the mates chose their watches, alternating the calls. Those selected by the first mate began to gather on the port side, while Barkley's selections gathered on the starboard. The two watches would be identified from here on as the Port or Starboard Watch.

When the selections were finished, all three of the shanghaied men were in Barkley's watch. Cade wasn't looking forward to being under Barkley, but he was glad that Pops and Stumpy were also a part of the Starboard Watch. He didn't think it was mere chance that he, Hernandez and Tait all wound up in Barkley's watch, and he mentioned it to Pops.

"It ain't just by chance at all," Pops said. "Anytime they's shanghaied sailors joinin' a crew, it's always the second mate that gets 'em."

With the watches selected, all eyes now turned toward the poop deck, waiting for the captain's order to make sail.

"Cap'n, watches tolled out 'n ready, sir!" the first mate shouted. Drake's voice, Cade thought, could probably be heard back on shore.

"Man the lee braces," Captain Mumford shouted in a voice that matched that of the first mate.

Some of the experienced crew were already at the brace belaying pin's on both sides of the ship, and they cast off the big coils of line, carefully capsizing them onto the deck so they would run free. It took less effort to haul around the heavy spars without the added weight of wind resistance on the sails, so bracing the yards first saved a great deal of hard labor.

"Lay aloft, you men," the second mate hollered indicating half a dozen members of his watch. "Castoff clew and bunt lines."

Pops, in his early fifties, was at home aloft. The first man to respond to the mate's orders, he ran up the mast easily. The others followed, including Cade. Reaching the yard, he stepped carefully onto the foot rope which immediately plunged 18 inches under his weight. He slid further out, trying to get a grip on the furled sail for support. The unyielding stiffness and weight of the canvas surprised him. When another sailor stepped out behind him, the foot rope jerked up under Cade's feet. He yelled as he clutched the sail trying to wrap his arms around its bulk. Even though the foot rope had evened out, it continued to snap back and forth, causing his legs to shake with fear and with the strain of trying to hold on.

Looking down some 65 feet, Cade heard Barkley shouting at them. He was inquiring whether they were going to just perch up there with their thumbs up their asses, or were they actually going to do some work? Then the orders began.

"Slack away clew and bunt lines!"

"Haul away Main and topsail sheets!"

"Haul away all jibs!"

"Belay for a main course tack!"

The open sails hung down, barely filled by the scant wind.

"To' gallant and royal gaskets off!"

Cade joined the others climbing farther up and inched out along the higher yards shaking off and coiling the light lines. He was up here with the others, and he knew he would have to do more than just hang on. His worst fear, even more intense than that of the height, was that he might disgrace himself. Yes he had been shanghaied, but he felt a real desire to be accepted by the crew.

All sails now hoisted and trimmed, and the spanker and its topsail in place, the FREMAD was under full sail, and headed south.

"Full and by," the captain ordered the helmsman.

With the ship now underway, the Starboard Watch, which was the off-watch was dismissed from duty. Standing down at the start of a passage also signaled the official beginning of the watch schedule. From that point on, they would alternate four hours on and four hours off, except for the two dog watches, which were each two hours long, from 4 to 6 in the afternoon and 6 to 8 in the evening. This would allow the crew to alter the night watches, so that no one was stuck permanently on the same schedule.

For the first couple of weeks of the voyage Cade found it hard to sleep because of the smoke, the changing of the watches, the constant noise from both above deck and below. The pitch and yaw of the vessel, which caused the hammock to swing, didn't help much. But by two weeks into the voyage exhaustion had rendered Cade oblivious to all, and nothing kept him awake.

He learned, quickly, that the routine of four hours on and four hours off meant that no one got more than three hours sleep at any one time, and most often considerably less than that. All of his personal business had to be done during his off watch. He had bought some clothes from the captain's slop chest, and though they were even more expensive than the new clothes he had bought back in Memphis, they were old, and he had to keep them in repair and this repair work took time away from sleeping. He had also bought oil skins to wear on deck against sea-spray. He looked like every other sailor on the boat.

In addition to the routine duties of self-maintenance, off time could be curtailed, or completely eliminated by the call of "All hands on deck!" That was a frequent necessity on this ship.

Pops was helpful, but Cade soon learned that Pops was pretty much a loner, who, while friendly to all, was friend with none. The rest of the crew had their own circles of three or four men, and they tended to maintain previously established relationships. It was quickly obvious that they weren't open to allowing anyone new into their little tight-knit assemblies.

That left the three new men to form their own mutual support group. Cade and Bento Hernandez had already become friends, swapping backgrounds as they worked or just visited in the fo'c'sle before collapsing into an exhausted sleep.

Bento, Cade learned, had come to Boston just prior to the Civil War. When the war started, he joined the navy, and was on board the KEERSAGE when that vessel sank the ALABAMA, which had been the Confederate States most effective war ship.

"We were on opposite sides during the war," Bento pointed out, when Cade shared some of his own war experiences.

"Yeah," Cade replied with a smile. "But you were in the navy and I was in the army, and I can guarantee you that we never fired one shot at each other."

Although both men tried to make friends with Tait, the young man was totally unable to adjust to his situation. A college student from Harvard, his father was a wealthy man in Boston, and had paid for Tait to take a vacation in exotic New Orleans.

"What does exotic mean?" Bento asked.

"It means different and glamorous," Tait explained. "I was in New Orleans for a week and while there, I stayed in the finest hotel, I ate in the finest restaurants, I enjoyed the most refined entertainment. But, I wanted to see the seamier side of the city before I went back to Boston, so I wandered down onto Canal Street and went into one of the bars."

"Tell me, Tait, did you happen to see an exotic woman in that bar?" Cade asked.

"I don't know. I don't remember anything beyond walking in. The next thing I knew, I woke up on this accursed ship."

"You should just try and make the best of it until we get back," Cade said. "I mean, really, when you think of it, what other choice do we have?"

"But my parents, they have no idea what happened to me. I know they are worried sick. This is wrong, this is so wrong."

By three weeks into the voyage, and with help from Bento and Pops, Cade had made a full adjustment to his circumstances, performing his duties as well as anyone else in the Starboard Watch. Tait was totally unable to adjust, and even though he tried, he remained a completely inept sailor. Barkley was vocal in his condemnation of the young man, cursing him constantly.

"Good money!" Barkley shouted at Tait. "We paid Lundy good money for you, you whimpering little bastard!"

Willoughby Tait was subjected to daily attacks by the rope's end, and two or three times per week would be tied to the main mast where, at the second mate's orders, the bo'sun would administer punishment, never more than twenty lashes, never less than ten. As a result, Tait's back was constantly covered by puffed up, purple, and often oozing welts.

"Mr. Barkley, I can't whip this boy no more," Higgins said. "He's had enough punishment."

"You'll lay on the lash, or I'll have you tied to the mast to take his punishment for him," Barkley said.

Then, two days before they were due to make anchor at the Rio de la Plata, the ship encountered very heavy weather, pounding through a rough sea with steep sided waves that threw spray as far back as the poop deck, and aloft almost to the foretop. Occasionally a wave would break over the bow and sweep across the low-slung main deck. The wind, which was quite high, tended to take the ship more east than the captain wanted to go, and the running had to be adjusted to compensate for that.

"Keep her full force, running with the wind," the captain ordered the helmsman.

It was the captain's intention to run with the gale so that the ship could build up maximum speed. That way he could swing back into the wind and use the ship's momentum to establish the tack.

"Ready about!" The captain ordered.

"All hands on deck to tack the ship! Ready about!" The first mate shouted, repeating the captain's order.

Cade, dealing with nausea in the rough sea, stumbled along the deck to the mainmast. The ship continued to plunge along to the southeast, steep waves crashing with such intensity that it sounded as if cannon balls were banging against the hull. The wind was loud and moaning in the web of rigging.

"Ready, sir!" The mate shouted up to the poop deck.

"Helmsman, ease it down," the captain ordered.

"Helm down, aye, aye, sir," the helmsman replied.

"Raise tacks and sheets!" The captain shouted

Seamen let go of the main lines then hauled the sails up by their clews so they would swing free. The ship came around, closer to the wind, with sails flopping and rattling, lines flailing, and masts vibrating. Cade could feel the pulsation in his feet through the deck.

The turn slowed as the sails lost the wind's force and the waves slapping and pounding on the weather side, resisted the vessel's pivot. Now the ship was almost head to the wind with all momentum lost.

When the captain sensed that the bowsprit was within a point or two of its head into the wind, he yelled the crucial order, "Mainsail haul!"

At once the seamen hauled hard and fast on the mainsail braces, Cade pulling as well, his nausea forgotten. The yard swung around with just enough momentum to bring the bow through so that the ship could push ahead, now with the help of the following waves.

"Starboard Watch, stand down," Barkley said, and rarely had Cade heard more welcome words.

Long Road to Abilene

12

THE STARBOARD WATCH caught a break in that their time on duty ended while the Port Watch, who had worked just as hard in trimming the ship to ride out the storm, had to remain on deck. Cade and the others were able to return to the fo'c'sle for some much needed rest.

"We'll be at the Plate by mid-mornin' tomorrow," Pops said. "We'll be off-loadin' some of our goods there, 'n pickin' up some tanned cowhides to take to California."

"Is the Plate a town?"

Pops shook his head. "It's a river," he said, "They call it Rio de la Plata. It separates Argentina from Uruguay."

"What city is there?"

"It's Buenos Aires, only we won't be dockin' there. Fact is, even with the tide in our favor, we can't get no closer 'n ten miles from the docks, on account of it's too shallow. What they do is, they send lighters out to the ship, 'n we put on them lighters what we're goin' to off load here, then some more lighters will be bringin' the hides out to us. It ain't nothin' at all like most ports o' call, bein' as there ain't no goin' ashore here, no liquor, no women, no nothin', but stayin on board the ship 'till all the work is done."

"Where is Tait?" Bento asked.

"Tait? I don't know, I haven't seen him since we stood down," Cade said. "Pops, Stumpy, have either of you seen him?"

Both men shook their heads.

"I seen 'im lyin' up on the fo'c'sle deck near the bo'sun's locker," one of the other sailors said.

"What do you mean you saw him lying there?" Cade asked. "You mean he was actually lying on the deck?"

"Yeah, that's what he was doin'."

"And you didn't say or do anything?"

"What did you want me to do? Turn 'im in? I figured he was just tryin' to hide from the second mate, seein' as how Barkley's been pickin' on 'im so much. Seemed to me the best thing to do was just let him stay there."

"That doesn't sound right. I'm going up to get him," Cade said.

"I'll go with you," Bento offered.

Cade and Bento scrambled up the companion ladder, and even though it had now grown quite dark, they were able to find the man lying just where the sailor told them he would be.

"Is he alive?" Bento asked.

When Cade touched him, Tait reacted.

"Please, don't hit me again," Tait begged. "Please, don't hurt me anymore."

"We're not going to hurt you, Willoughby," Cade said. "We're here to help you."

With Cade on one side, and Bento on the other, the two men helped Tait to the companion ladder way. Cade went down first, then Bento lowered Tait from above, and Cade took him from below so that the two of them managed to get the boy down, and into his own hammock. The back of Tait's shirt was red with blood, and when Cade tried to take it off, Tait cried out in pain.

Cade had to cut the shirt off in strips.

"My God!" Pops said when he saw Tait's back. "I been at sea, man and boy for over thirty years, 'n I ain't never seen nothin' this bad."

There was no part of Tait's actual skin that could be seen. His back was nothing but bloody welts.

"Stumpy, take a pail up 'n scoop up some salt water," Pops said. "We need to clean this boy's back."

"Aye, aye," Stumpy replied, just as if he had been given the order by one of the ship's officers.

Half an hour later the blood had been washed away, but the wounds still looked just as bad.

"I got some creosote in my sea-bag," Pops said. "We'll put some o' that on him. That'll ease the pain somewhat, 'n also keep the wounds from putrifyin'."

"There's no way he'll be able to make watch tonight, or even tomorrow mornin'," one of the other sailors said.

"It won't matter that much tonight," Pops said as, very gently, he applied the black substance, spreading it evenly over Tait's back. "There won't be no sail changes to make, so 'bout the only thing we'll have to do is be on deck. And Barkley sleeps through most of the night watches anyhow, so he'll never notice. But we'll be on watch 'bout the time the first lighter gets here, 'n I don't see no way this boy will be up to helpin' us off-load the grain. Barkley will for sure notice it then."

"Maybe if we all just take it up a notch, 'n get all the work done without 'im, Barkley won't even know," Stumpy suggested.

"He'll know," Pops said. "I don't know why, but he's got it in just real special for that boy."

"We'll just have to see what happens tomorrow," Cade said.

The FREMAD dropped anchor at nine –thirty-five the next morning, which was thirty - one days after leaving New Orleans. At this point they were ten miles off-shore from the mouth of the Rio de la Plata, so far that the land was little more than a thin and irregular line on the distant horizon.

When the lighter came alongside, all hands were called on deck to begin unloading the grain that was being delivered here.

The lighter had brought fresh beef and sweet potatoes with it, and as the men worked to move grain from the hold of the FREMAD to the deck of the flat hulled scow, the smell of cooking beef permeated the ship. The men worked eagerly, anxious for their first real meal in over a month.

It took an hour and a half for the barge to be loaded, then with its cargo, the lighter started for shore. The FREMAD'S time here wasn't over, however. Before it could leave anchorage, it would have to take on ten tons of tanned cowhides for shipment to San Francisco. The barge with the cowhides had come out to the FREMAD at the same time as the lighter which just left. During the morning it had been anchored one hundred yards abeam the starboard, patiently awaiting its turn to come alongside.

"Mr. Drake, give the men half an hour for lunch," Captain Mumford ordered.

"Aye, aye, sir," Drake replied.

The men went happily to the galley. Cade petitioned the cook to provide him with an extra bowl to take to Willoughby Tait.

"Ifen he wants to eat, he'll come here 'n eat it like ever' one else," the cook said.

"He can't come," Cade said. "He's too badly hurt."

"Hurt? How'd he get hurt? I ain't heard o' no one havin' no accident."

"He's been too badly beaten."

The cook shook his head. "There ain't hardly no sailor at all that I know of who ain't felt the lash a time or two. I can't be doin' no special favors for someone just 'cause he ain't man enough to stand up to a little punishment. Now get on with you."

Cade had his meal in his bowl and he started toward the table then he stopped.

"What are you going to do, Pogue?" Bento asked, still referring to Cade by the name he had learned.

"I'm going to take half my dinner to Tait."

"I'll take half of mine, as well."

"No, you'll give him one third of yours, I'll give him one third of mine, and that way, we'll all three have two thirds."

Hernandez smiled and nodded his head.

When they reached the fo'c'sle a few minutes later, Tait was lying on his side in his hammock.

"How are you doing?" Cade said.

"I can't lie on my back."

"Well, hell, you wouldn't want to anyway. Pops smeared your back with some black concoction and all you would do is get your hammock dirty. You wouldn't want to sleep in a dirty hammock, would you?" Cade teased.

Tait smiled. "I guess not."

"We brought you something to eat."

Tait shook his head. "Thanks, but I don't think I can eat another bite of salt pork."

"Who said anything about salt pork? Take a sniff of this," Cade said.

Tait raised himself up and Cade held the bowl under his nose.

"What is that? Fresh beef? How did we . . ."

"We're anchored off the coast of Argentina, and the lighter brought it aboard."

"We're in port?"

Laboriously, and with help, Tait climbed out of his hammock. "Pogue, here is our opportunity! We could go ashore and see the American consulate here. We could get word to my father and he would send us enough money to get back home."

"You don't understand, when I say off the coast, I mean at least ten miles off coast," Cade said. "We can't get any closer because the water is too shallow."

"Where is your bowl? Bento asked. "I am hungry and want to eat."

"Do you feel up to sitting at the card table? We can eat there," Cade suggested.

"Yes, I can sit there."

Tait found his bowl, and at the card table, Cade and Bento apportioned the meals. As Cade hoped it would, the food seemed to make Tait feel better, and he even began to share more of himself.

"There is something I haven't told either of you," Tait said. "I haven't spoken of it before, because the irony is just too bitter to contemplate."

"Irony?" Bento replied.

"The . . . bitter absurdity," Tait said. "I told you my father is a wealthy man in Boston. What I didn't tell you is that he owns a shipping company." Tait waved his hand, taking in the ship. "And now, here I am, a common sailor on a ship just like the dozen or so he owns."

"Tait Shipping Company?" Bento said. "I shipped out once on the SUCCESS."

"Yes! That's one of my father's ships!" Tait said, showing more animation than he had at any time since coming on board. He laughed. "You know what; this might turn out to be a good thing. One day I will probably own that company. And because of my experience on this ship, I will make certain that everyone who sails for me will be fairly treated."

"Well, Bento and I need to get back to work," Cade said when they finished eating.

"Maybe I had better try and come with you," Tait suggested.

"Don't be silly. In your condition you would just get in the way," Cade said.

* * *

They heard someone coming down the ladder and looking toward it, saw that it was the second mate.

"Here you are, you malingerin' bastards," Barkley said. "It's time to get back to work."

"We're going," Cade said, as he and Bento started toward the ladder.

"You didn't repair for duty this morning, did you?" Barkley said, walking over to the table where Tait was still sitting. "It's to the mast with you . . .you sniveling son of a bitch, and thirty lashes this time."

Cade, who by now had reached the foot of the ladder, turned back toward the second mate.

"Are you insane, Barkley? He's in no condition to work, and thirty lashes would kill him."

"Then I'll just take care of him here," Barkley growled.

Both Cade and Bento started back toward the table where Tait was sitting, defenseless before Barkley's assault. Cade didn't notice until it was too late that Barkley was carrying a bludgeon. When Cade reached for him, Barkley whirled around, the club striking Cade just above his ear. Cade went down.

"BASTARDO!" Bento shouted, just before Barkley turned the club on him as well.

Now, with neither Cade nor Bento able to interfere, Barkley turned all his attention, and his fury on the boy who sat helpless before him.

"You have been nothing but trouble ever since you were brought aboard!" Barkley said, hitting Tait in the face with his club. The blow broke Tait's nose, and it began to bleed. Tait cried out and put both hands in front of his face. That seemed to anger Barkley even more, and he brought the club down with even more force on Tait's head, and Tait collapsed onto the table.

Cade managed to get to his feet, and seeing a broken belaying pin on the deck near the bulkhead, he grabbed it.

"Barkley," Cade said. "Leave the boy alone!"

With a loud, guttural yell, Barkley raised his club and charged Cade. Cade stepped to one side, like a matador teasing a bull, then he brought the belaying pin down on the second mate's head with as much force as he could muster. Barkley collapsed.

"Willoughby!" Cade shouted, and he hurried to the boy's inert form.

Tait groaned.

"Thank God you're alive."

"I don't feel like I'm alive," Tait said.

"Barkley's dead," Bento said from his squatting position by the second mate's body.

"You'd better get out of here, fast," Cade said. "There's no way the captain is going to believe that you had no hand in this."

"I do have a hand in this, Pogue," Bento replied.

"He's right, he did have a hand in it," a third voice said, and Cade saw Pops standing at the foot of the ladder. "And now, so do I."

"Pops! When did you get here?" Cade asked.

"I've been here long enough to know that you were right in what you did. But Barkley was an officer, and the word of an ordinary seaman ain't goin' to keep either one of you from bein' hung. You're both goin' to have to run."

"Run? How are we going to run? We're ten miles off shore."

"You let me handle that," Pops said. He looked down at Barkley's body. "First thing we're goin' to have to do is get rid of this son of a bitch."

"What are we going to do with him?"

"We'll put 'im in the bo'sun's locker, it's far enough forward that nobody will see us, 'n it'll more 'n like be several hours a'fore he's found. By that time you two will be gone."

Bento was the first one to the body, and he stuck his hand into Barkley's pocket, then brought out a wad of currency.

"Look," he said holding it up. "He had forty dollars!"

"That's good," Pops said. "Five dollars will get the two of you ashore, but you'd better hang on to the rest 'cause you're goin' to be a' needin' it."

13

"BEFORE WE MOVE HIM, we need to get Willoughby back in his hammock."

"Do you think he'll be . . ."

"All right? Yeah, especially now that Barkley won't be hitting him anymore. He's going to have a headache and a sore back for a few days, but I'll take care of him."

"I owe you my life, Pogue," Tait said. "I think Barkley would have killed me."

"Listen, maybe it's time I told all of you something. My name isn't Pogue Copley, it's Cade McCall. I've got a brother, Adam, in Clarksville, Tennessee. If I don't get off this ship alive, I'd like someone to get word to him."

"I understand," Pops said.

After hiding Barkley's body, Cade, Bento, and Pops went to mid-deck. They were the first ones there, the crew was still enjoying their meal in the galley, while the captain, Mr. Drake, and Bo'sun Higgins had not yet left the officer's dining salon. The scow was tied alongside, and the three men of its crew were sitting on one of the bundles of cowhides, waiting to transfer their cargo to the FREMAD.

"Give me five dollars," Pops said.

Bento gave him a bill, and Pops climbed down into the barge, then engaged the boat master in a conversation that required many gestures and a lot of pointing. Finally the lighter master nodded his head, and took the proffered money.

Shortly after that, the work party returned, followed a moment later by the captain, the first mate, and the bo'sun.

"Burke, what are you doin' down there?" the first mate asked.

"These here fellers was askin' if they could have three men come down here to help 'em with the loadin'," Pops replied.

"Sure, grab a couple more," Drake said.

"Copley, Hernandez, you're in the Starboard Watch, climb down here," Pops ordered, and quickly, the two men responded.

"Speaking of the Starboard Watch, where is Mr. Barkley?" Captain Mumford asked.

"I ain't seen 'im since he got up from the dinner table," the bo'sun said.

"Well, until he shows up, you're in charge of his watch."

"Aye, aye, sir."

For the next half hour, Cade, Bento, Pops, and the three lighter crewmen began cutting down the size of the cargo that had been brought out. For the entire time they worked, Cade worried that someone was going to discover Barkley's body in the bo'sun's locker. Then, shortly before the last four bundles were passed up, the captain of the lighter signaled that Cade and Bento should get into the engine room, and this they did.

Not until they were a mile or so away from the FREMAD did the two come out onto the deck.

When they drew alongside the lighter that had taken the grain from the FREMAD, Cade saw that it was anchored at least three miles off shore, and still three-quarters filled with the bags of grain. Then he saw a very strange thing, horses, hip-deep in water, were drawing high-wheeled carts out to the anchored boat.

"That's the damndest thing I've ever seen," Cade said, pointing to the carts. "Why is that barge anchored so far off shore?"

"A heavily loaded boat draws too much water to get any closer, so they have to bring these carts out here to off-load them," Bento said.

"Are we going to have to get into one of those carts?"

"No. This lighter is empty so it is riding high enough in the water that we can go ashore."

"Ashore, yeah," Cade said. "So what do we do then?"

Exactly what they were going to do came to a head the next morning when they were surprised to see Stumpy Jones.

"Bento, look," Cade said, pointing to the man who, but the day before, had been a fellow seaman. "What is he doing ashore?"

"I think he is looking for us," Bento replied.

"Do you see anyone else with him?"

"No."

Cade looked around very carefully, then seeing no other familiar faces, called out.

"Stumpy?"

Stumpy came quickly to them.

"Are you looking for us?" Cade asked.

"Aye. I came ashore with Billy Boggs 'n the bo'sun. Only Higgins ain't the bo'sun no more. He's the second mate."

"Higgins is the second mate?"

'Yeah, they found Barkley's body."

Cade nodded. "I figured they would."

"The cap'n has put out a five hunnert dollar reward for you two," Stumpy said. "You'd better not stay here, everyone in Buenos Aires is going to be wanting to collect that money and it won't be that hard for 'em to pick you two out, especially with your red hair,"

"How's Tait doing?" Cade asked.

"He's comin' along. And Higgins, bein' the new second mate, says Tait won't be gettin' no more punishment. By the way, the boy 'n Pops both told the cap'n what happened, and that you two didn' have no choice. But bein' as Barkley was an officer, the cap'n says he don't have no choice neither, but to try 'n bring you in."

"I see you're wearing a pistol," Cade said. "You aren't going to try and take us in, are you?"

"No. Pops got me onto the shore party so's I could find you 'n warn you. You two has got to get out of here."

"Thanks, Stumpy," Cade said.

"I should thank you. The whole crew should thank you for killin' that son of a bitch. Listen, I heard somethin' that might help. There's an Italian gunboat here that's goin' up the Paraguay River to Matto Grosso, it's like a state in north Brazil. They's some Italians 'n other foreign folks up there, and this boat is goin' to pick 'em up 'n take 'em out, on account of the war."

"What war?"

"There's some kind of war goin' on here, 'n they say it's just plumb awful," Stumpy said. "Anyway, if I was you two, I'd be figurin' out some way to be gettin' on that boat a' fore it leaves."

"There's Boggs," Bento said, pointing out the other sailor.

Boggs saw the three of them, and with a nod, warned that Higgins was nearby.

"I'd better be a' gettin'," Stumpy said.

"I have an idea," Cade said after Stumpy left. "He said this Italian boat was going up-river to evacuate some foreigners. If we tell the captain that we have some people up there, he may let us buy passage."

* * *

"No, I cannot sell you passage," the boat captain said. He studied Cade and Bento for a moment. "You are dressed as sailors. Are you sailors?"

Cade hesitated for a moment before answering. He was certain that word was already out that two sailors were wanted fugitives.

"Because if you are, I'm a few men short, and I would be willing to take you up river as part of my crew."

"Captain, you've got a deal," Cade said, extending his hand.

Once the lines were cast off and the anchor raised, there was little for any of the crew to do as the boat proceeded up the Rio de la Plata River. Unlike the boats Cade had experienced on the Tennessee, Ohio, and Mississippi rivers, this boat, the SOLARI, used a screw, rather than paddle wheels for propulsion.

Cade couldn't help but compare the Rio de la Plata with the Mississippi. The Mississippi was broad and majestic, flowing by planted fields and stately homes. The Plate River was untamed with tangled growth crowding down to its banks. Often animals that were strange to Cade would emerge from the encroaching forest to drink from the river. Brightly colored birds flitted about, filling the air with calls that were louder even that the steam engine that propelled the SOLARI upstream.

There were eight 32 pounder Whitworth guns on the boat, four on either side.

Oliver Cabot was the only Englishman on board, and Cade made his acquaintance shortly after they got underway. Cabot was a geologist who was trying to get back to the diamond fields at Diamantino.

"Diamonds? You mean real diamonds, like the jewels?"

"Well, eventually," Cabot replied with a little smile. "They don't look like much when you first see them. They have to be cut and polished before some lady would allow them to be put around her neck."

"Why did you leave?"

"The war, dear boy, the war," Cabot replied.

"Yes, I heard someone say something about a war." Cade pointed to the cannon. "Are we likely to get involved?"

"I wouldn't think so," Cabot replied. "This boat is Italian, I'm British, you are American and your friend is Portuguese. There is not a person on board who is from a belligerent country, so by the rules of war, we will be able to pass safely through to pick up other non-belligerents and take them to safety. As mad as Lopez is, I don't expect even he would interfere."

"Who is Lopez?"

"General Francisco Solano Lopez is the president of Paraguay. He is also a madman and because of that, totally unpredictable. The really bizarre thing is, he is as big a threat to his own people as is the enemy."

"Yeah, I was at Franklin, during the war. I've had some experience of generals making bad decisions."

"I have read of that battle," Cabot said. "I don't think either general was very smart that day, but at least Generals Hood and Schofield didn't murder their own men."

Cade started to refute him, remembering that at Franklin the Federal troops fired grape and canister, indiscriminately, killing many of their own troops who were massed so closely with the attacking Confederates. But he knew this wasn't what Cabot meant.

"Wait a minute, you aren't just talking about bad decisions here, are you?"

"No, I'm talking about murder."

"Are you saying he has actually murdered some of his own people?"

"Let me tell you a story that is widely known. In a recent battle the Paraguayan general was engaged with Brazilian troops that outnumbered him four to one. He managed to withdraw without losing his entire command, and he sent his adjutant and two others to take the report to Lopez."

"I take it Lopez was disappointed at the outcome?"

Cabot made a scoffing sound. "Disappointed? Disappointed, dear boy? Yes, you might say that. He was so disappointed that he executed the adjutant and the two who had come with him."

"Yeah, I'd say that's a little more than a bad decision."

"Then when the Tenth Battalion returned, the first to do so, he executed the commander, and every tenth man of the battalion."

"Damn!" Cade said. "I've run across some evil men in my day but I've never known, or even heard of anyone to match this Lopez."

"Nor have I," Cabot said. "So now you can see why I said that he is as big a threat to his own army, as is the enemy."

At nine o'clock the next morning Cade, Bento, Cabot, and nearly the entire crew were on deck as the boat passed by the town of Humaita. This, the captain of the gunship had been told, was the main stronghold of the entire Paraguayan army. There were several Paraguayan soldiers on the bank of the river, and those on the deck of the SOLARI waved at them. None of the soldiers returned the waves.

"They don't seem like a very friendly bunch," Cade said.

"They are probably too frightened of Lopez to wave," Cabot replied.

"That looks like a Monitor," Bento said, pointing to an ironclad boat that lay tied up to one of the docks. The deck of the boat was low, only inches above the water. The turret stuck up from the middle of the boat, like an observation turret.

"I'm surprised to see that Paraguay has such a warship," Cabot said. "I thought only the Brazilian navy had them."

"The name says it is the ALGOAS," Bento said. "It IS Brazilian."

"Interesting. They must have captured it."

At that moment the SOLARI came to a sudden stop, so severe that many on board were thrown into the water. The unexpected stop was accompanied by a loud noise, as if the boat had collided with something, but there was nothing visible in the water ahead.

Cade and Cabot had been thrown to the deck at the impact. Bento, who was holding on to the railing at the time avoided being thrown into the water. Bento reached down to help both Cade and Cabot to their feet.

"What the hell happened?" Cade asked. "What would make us stop like that?"

"VI È UNA CATENA IN ACQUA!" one of the Italian crewmen who was near the bow of the boat shouted. "VI È UNA CATENA IN ACQUA!"

"What is he saying?" Cade asked.

"There is a chain in the river, stretched from one side to the other," Cabot said. "We hit the chain."

"What's a chain doing there?" Bento asked.

"It looks like we are about to find out," Cade said, pointing to more than a dozen boats, each filled with soldiers, paddling rapidly to where the SOLARI sat, dead in the water.

"Whatever they want, we're helpless to deal with them," Cabot said. "Except for the cannon we have no arms aboard. And we have no powder and shells for the cannon, because that would be a violation of our neutrality."

"Maybe once they see that we are no threat, they'll take down the chain and let us pass," Cade suggested.

"Look at the expression on the face of the officer in the lead boat," Cabot said. "I don't think magnanimity is on their minds."

14

THE PARAGUAYAN SOLDIERS put everyone on the Italian gunboat in shackles, then took them ashore. There the crew of the SOLARI was ordered to line up in one long line, the captain and first mate at the head of the line, then every uniformed sailor beside him.

Because Cade, Bento, and Cabot were not in the uniform of the Italian navy, they were separated from the sailors. A Paraguayan officer read aloud, from a paper.

"What is he saying, Bento?"

"He says that the Italian sailors have invaded Paraguay, and they are to be executed."

"No!" Cabot shouted. "You can't do this! These men are from a neutral country, they have every right to evacuate their countrymen from a war zone!"

The Paraguayan officer paid no attention to Cabot's outburst. As soon as he finished reading the execution orders, twenty-three soldiers, one for each Italian sailor, marched out, turned to face the line of prisoners, raised their rifles to their shoulders and aimed.

"FUEGO!" the Paraguayan officer ordered.

All twenty-three rifles discharged as one, and the captain and his entire crew went down. The soldiers then walked over to the sailors who were on the ground and began stabbing and hacking at the fallen men with the bayonets attached to the end of their rifles.

The Paraguayan officer then came over to address Cade, Bento, and Cabot. He started to speak, but Cabot interrupted him.

"I know you speak English. If you have anything to say to us, say it in English," he demanded.

"You are the geologist in the diamond field, aren't you?" the officer replied.

"Yes."

"Who are these men?"

"They are a part of my personal staff, and they enjoy the protection of Her Majesty, Queen Victoria. Your President has visited our Queen. If you shoot any of us, you will displease the Queen, and that will displease President Lopez."

The officer stroked his chin for a moment, then spoke in Spanish to one of his soldiers.

"You have no right to put us in prison, either," Cabot said, having understood the officer's order. You have the obligation, not only to let us go, but to provide us with safe transport to Diamantina."

"For now, you will be our guests," the officer said.

As the door was shut and locked behind the three men, Cade could only think, 'NOT AGAIN!' The walls were made of stone blocks, the windows, like the door, were barred. There was no furniture of any kind in the room, no bunks, no chairs, no benches. There weren't even any blankets or padding. They would have to sleep on the floor.

"I'm not staying here," Cade said.

"I must admit that the accommodations leave much to be desired," Cabot said. "But I'm not sure we can just check out because we are unsatisfied with our room."

"I'm not staying here," Cade said again. He sat down and leaned his back against the stone wall, studying both the barred door and the windows.

Approximately an hour after they had been put into their cell, they heard a lot of shouting outside. Then, surprisingly, they heard the screams and cries of women and children.

"Bento, what is that all about? What's going on?" Cade asked.

"The Fifth Corps of Paraguay Reserves has been defeated by the Argentinians," Bento said, translating what he had heard. "Sixteen hundred of the two thousand men were killed, the others captured."

"The women? Who are the women that we hear crying?"

"They are the wives and children of the soldiers of the soldiers of the Fifth Corps."

For the next several minutes Cade listened to the shouting and the wailing. He was sympathetic to the women who had lost their husbands but, for the moment, he was even more concerned with his own plight. Having been a prisoner at Camp Douglas was bad, but he always knew that when the war ended, he would be released. He had no such assurance here.

"My God," Cabot suddenly said. "They are going to kill them."

"What? Kill who?"

"The women and children," Cabot said. "They just got the order from Lopez to kill the women and children as punishment because their husbands failed in their mission."

A few minutes later the door to their cell was jerked open.

"FUERA, FUERA, SALIR AHORA," one of the three armed men shouted.

"What is he saying?" Cade asked.

"They want us to come out," Cabot said.

"Good, maybe they are going to let us go."

"No," Bento said somberly. "They are going to kill the women and the children, then they are going to kill us."

Cade and the others were taken out to the plaza, where the crew of the SOLARI had been killed earlier. He saw scores of women standing in the middle of the plaza, in some cases women holding infant children in their arms, in other cases children standing at their mother's side, clinging to them. The expression of the faces of the children ranged from fear to confusion. Strangely, Cade thought, many of the women seemed to show an almost detached acceptance of what was about to happen.

Three more men, also prisoners, were brought over to stand beside Cade, Bento, and Cabot. Bento exchanged a few words with them.

"They are crewmen of the monitor that was captured," Bento explained.

A Paraguayan officer ordered several of his men to spread out in front of the women and children and, just as they had when they executed the crew of the SOLARI, the soldiers took aim.

The officer shouted at the women, and Cabot translated.

"Your men were cowards. They failed the president and the country. Most have been killed, so they cannot be punished. You will be punished in their place."

Cade noticed then, that there were only three men guarding them, and all three were more interested in what was about to happen with the women and children, than they were with the men prisoners that were in their charge.

"God help us for taking advantage of such an awful thing," Cade said in English. "But when the shooting starts, I think we might have a chance to overpower the guards."

"Yes," Cabot agreed.

"Bento, tell the Brazilians to be ready."

Bento spoke very quietly to the three sailors from the monitor, and Cade saw them nod in agreement.

"FUEGO!" the Paraguayan officer shouted, and gunfire erupted. The three who were supposed to be guarding Cade watched in fascination as the bullets tore into the women and children.

"Now!" Cade shouted.

There were six prisoners to three guards, and though the guards were armed, they weren't attentive. They were quickly overpowered and relieved of their rifles. Cade now had one of the rifles, and when the solider he had taken it from tried to shout out, Cade made a vicious butt stroke into the guard's face, and he saw several teeth fly out as the man went down.

Bento also had one of the rifles, but the third rifle wound up in the hands of one of the Brazilian sailors. The Brazilian bayoneted all three of the guards.

While the execution of the women and children continued, Cade and the others made good their escape, hurrying down to the river where the Brazilians led them onto the ALGOAS. By the time Cade and the others boarded the little armored craft, the Paraguayan colonel realized what was happening, and he ordered his soldiers in pursuit.

The retaining ropes were loosed, and as the boat began to drift out into the middle of the river, Cade and the others climbed down inside, and closed the hatch.

The pursuing soldiers, more than a hundred of them, got into boats and paddled after the ALGOAS. At the moment, the monitor was without power so the soldiers were able to overtake it quickly and scramble aboard.

"We need to get this thing going," Cade said. "They're climbing over us like piss ants on a lump of sugar."

"It will take a few minutes to get up steam pressure," Cabot replied.

On deck they could hear the soldiers shouting, and pounding on the metal door that secured the hatch.

"Ask the Brazilians if they think the hatch will hold," Cade said.

"It will hold," one of the sailors replied in English.

"Ah, good, we can talk."

Suddenly a smoking black object was dropped in through the opening on the turret.

"It's a hand grenade!" Cabot shouted.

With the sputtering fuse quickly getting shorter, Cade picked it up and tossed it back through the little opening. It exploded on deck, and the shouts from outside suggested that some of the soldiers had been wounded from their own grenade.

Cade climbed up to give him access to the opening so he could see what was going on. Then, he realized that he could use the opening as a gun port. The rifle he had taken from the guard was a Henry Repeating Rifle, and Cade began firing through the port with deadly effect. The soldiers on the flat deck had nothing to provide cover, and three of them went down before the others could get out of the line of fire.

The turret housed a 70 pounder cannon, but upon being captured all the ammunition had been removed. The turret could swing around, however, which meant that no matter where the sailors were on deck, Cade could engage them.

"TEMOS A PRESSÃO DO VAPOR!" one of the Brazilians shouted, happily.

"We have steam pressure," Bento translated.

"Good! Let's get the hell out of here!" Cade replied.

Once the little armored boat got underway the few Paraguayan soldiers who had remained on deck jumped into the water to be picked up by those in the boats and Cade saw the boats paddling away, quickly.

"They're leaving!" he said. "They're giving up on us."

Cade spoke too soon, for less than a minute later, there was a tremendous crashing sound from outside. Turning the turret to see what was happening, he saw the simultaneous flash of several cannon from the shore.

As they pulled away slowly, solid ball and explosive shell slammed into armored covering of the boat, and though the noise inside was deafening, they sustained no serious damage. Within fifteen minutes they were out of range and continuing up river.

Three days later the ALGOAS put ashore.

"The river will not allow us to go any farther," Osorio said. Osorio was the senior of the three sailors, and the only one who could speak English.

"You have our thanks," Cade said.

"No, SENHOR, we thank you. We owe you our lives," Osorio said.

There was an Indian village near the river's edge and it required but little negotiation to arrange for a canoe to take them the rest of the way up the Paraguay River until they literally ran out of water.

"What do we do now?" Cade asked, as they watched the canoe paddle back downriver.

Cabot smiled. "A horse, a horse, my kingdom for a horse. Or, with apologies to Mr. Shakespeare, a mule, a mule, my kingdom for a mule."

"I don't have a kingdom to trade, but right now a horse or a mule would be good," Cade said.

"Fortunately, gentlemen, we don't need a kingdom. Mr. Gundar will furnish us with mules for just a few coin of the realm."

Cade had never seen anyone with skin as wrinkled as Mr. Gundar. There was not one half inch of smooth surface anywhere on his body. He had no teeth, so his cheeks were sunken in, and his chin protruded so that it looked almost as if it could touch his nose. He was very thin, and very short, barely over five feet tall.

It was obvious that he and Cabot knew each other, and after a few words he appeared with four mules, one of which he would ride so that, when they reached Diamantino, Gundar could bring his mules back.

Six Months Later:

Cade and Bento were having dinner with Cabot and Serafina, the beautiful Brazilian woman who shared his home. During the previous six months, both Cade and Bento had worked alongside Cabot as he explored other potential areas for mining diamonds. The diamonds were readily accessible, some found along stream banks or just lying on top of the ground, and any that were found in such a way, Cabot let Cade and Bento keep. The working mines were owned by the state, and Africans did all the labor.

The cook had prepared turtle soup and manioc bread, which they enjoyed with sarsaparilla tea.

"Must you leave tomorrow?" Serafina asked. "I so hate to see the two of you go."

"South America has been quite interesting, and, except for the first few weeks we were here, I've very much enjoyed it," Cade said. "But I have been gone well over a year. I'm really anxious to get back, especially now that Oliver has allowed me to earn a little money."

"You deserve it. I would be dead if it weren't for your initiative," Cabot said. "I think you both should be leaving with about seven hundred fifty dollars in American money. Try not to exchange more diamonds than you have to here in Brazil. The natives often find diamonds and turn them in for farina, and I'm afraid some of the local dealers are not very scrupulous."

"I have to exchange a few before I can buy passage for America. Is there someone you can recommend?" Cade asked.

"Captain Hislop. He's been around these parts for at least fifteen or twenty years, and he can be trusted, for all that he's a Scotsman," Cabot said with a little chuckle. "You'll find him when you get to Santarem, but first you have to get there."

"You say that like it might be difficult," Bento said.

Both Seraphina and Cabot smiled. "Just remember to close your eyes when your guide pushes his little canoe into the rapids," Cabot said. "I'll go with you to the headwaters of the Tapajos tomorrow and make sure the Matses guide you hire is a competent one."

"I appreciate that," Cade said. "How long do you think it will take us to get to Santa Maria de Belem?"

"It's going to take at least six months to get to the Atlantic."

"Yes, but once you leave from Santarem, it should be a delightful trip," Seraphina added as she rose from the table. "I have a present for each of you."

"Oh, Seraphina, you didn't have to do that," Cade said. "You and Oliver have been more than generous for the whole time we have been here."

"Wait," she said, holding up her finger. She returned a moment later with two string hammocks. "When you're floating down the Amazon, you'll enjoy having these to lie in as you watch the coffee, rubber, and orange trees go by. Why, who knows, you may decide that you don't want to go back to the States."

"I'm definitely going back to the States, but who knows? Maybe someday I'll return."

15

CADE AND BENTO HAD SEPARATED at Santa Maria de Belem. Bento wanted to go back to Boston, not only to tell Jefferson Tait where his son was, but also to reconnect with family and friends he had left there. Ironically, Bento would be sailing on a Tait ship, the ENTERPRISE, and not as a passenger, but as an able-bodied seaman, having signed on as such.

Cade booked passage on the steamship LOYALIST, which left four days after the ENTERPRISE, and though it was primarily a cargo ship, it did have accommodations for passengers. On March 15th, 1867' which was one year, seven months and eight days after Cade had left New Orleans as a shanghaied sailor on board the FREMAD, the LOYALIST docked in New Orleans.

"It has been a pleasure having you aboard, Mr. McCall," the purser said as Cade left the ship.

"Thank you," Cade said. "Please extend my compliments to the captain and the crew for making the passage a pleasant one."

Cade was anxious to convert his diamonds into cash. Cabot had appraised them at approximately 750 dollars, though he did caution him that the market would vary.

The first thing Cade did was check into a hotel at the corner of St. Louis and Chartres. This was the same hotel he had stayed in the last time he was in New Orleans, though it had been for one night only, his time in New Orleans having been truncated by events.

"Do you have a city directory?" Cade asked as he was signing the register.

"Indeed we do, sir. You will find it on that desk," the clerk replied, pointing to the object as he spoke. "We ask that you examine it here, in the lobby, though, and not take it to your room."

"That'll be fine," Cade said.

Before he even went up to his room, he went over to the desk and began perusing the directory. It took less than a minute to find what he was looking for:

Culpepper Investment Services: Stock, Land, Gold, Gems
327 Bourbon Street

"Oh that's quite easy to find, sir," the clerk said when Cade asked directions. "You just go up St. Louis Street for three blocks, then turn left on Bourbon. They have a nice sign out front, you can't miss it."

Ten minutes later, Cade was talking to the investment broker. The broker's response to Cade saying he wanted to sell some diamonds was almost dismissive.

"Sir, if you have a diamond pendant or jewel of some kind, I really think you would be better off selling it to a jeweler, or perhaps to a pawnbroker."

Cade shook his head. "I'm not talking about that kind of diamonds." Cade was carrying a small leather pouch, and he poured the contents onto the broker's desk.

"Oh my!" the broker said, looking at the raw diamonds. "We don't often see this fine a specimen. Where did you come by these?"

"I'm just off the boat from Brazil."

"Well, they are marvelous."

"Do you think you can handle them?"

"Yes, I'm sure we can."

After weighing the diamonds, then assessing each one individually, the broker stepped to one side and discussed the offer with one of the other brokers. Cade had decided to stand firm at seven hundred dollars, keeping in mind Cabot's suggestion that he should realize around seven hundred fifty dollars.

The broker returned.

"We are prepared to offer you thirteen hundred and fifty dollars," he said. "Admittedly they would be worth more in New York or Boston, but we are in New Orleans."

Cade wanted to laugh out loud, but he restrained himself, and with a quiet, and he hoped, reserved, nod he replied.

"I'll take it."

The broker smiled. "We'll write you a bank draft."

"I am going to be traveling, I would prefer the money in cash."

"I'm afraid we don't have that much cash on hand."

"There is a bank across the street."

The broker sighed. "Very well, if you will wait here, I'll send our Mr. Peabody to the bank to withdraw the funds."

"Thank you."

Half an hour later Cade was enjoying his dinner in Antoine's. He thought about the money he now had on his person, which, ironically, was almost the same amount he had with him the last time he came to New Orleans. The only difference was, he had come by this money legally.

As he thought about the money he had lost here, he remembered the person that he was certain had taken it:

Chantal. And after he finished his meal, he planned to pay her a visit.

He smiled as he anticipated the expression on her face when he confronted her.

Topping off his meal with a glass of claret, Cade returned to the Lafitte's Blacksmith Shop Bar. As before, the bar was filled with seamen and river boatman, but whereas the first time the appearance and patois of the seamen had been relatively strange to him, this time there was a very strong familiarity. It took very little imagination for him to put himself, once more, hanging in the braces, or in the fo'c'sle of the FREMAD.

A very attractive young woman approached him.

"You don't look like a sailor," she said, and indeed, Cade had abandoned his seaman's attire even before he boarded the ENTERPRISE.

"That's because I'm not a sailor," he said.

The young woman, who had long blonde hair and flashing blue eyes, smiled broadly. "That's all right, you are welcome here, anyway. My name is Delight."

"Delight, is it? Tell me, Delight, would Chantal be here by any chance?"

Delight looked confused. "Chantal? No, there is nobody here by the name of Chantal."

"Oh," Cade said, the expression in his voice showing his obvious disappointment.

"Did you know a Chantal here?"

"Yes, I met her the last time I was here, about a year and a half ago."

"I've only been here for about six months, but wait. Eddie, the bartender has been here forever. If you'll wait here for a moment I'll see if he knows anything about her."

"Thank you."

"Galveston," Delight said when she came back.

"Galveston?"

"Eddie said she just up and quit one day about eighteen months or so ago. Said she was going to Galveston. But I'm here, honey."

"Yeah," Cade said, smiling at the thought. "Yeah, I guess you are."

Delight was the first woman Cade had been with since Chantal, and though it was enjoyable, it didn't take very long. He was back downstairs within half an hour, and stepping up to the bar, ordered a beer.

"Delight tells me that you said Chantal had gone to Galveston."

"That's right," the bartender said as he made a few swipes of the bar with a damp cloth.

"Do you know where she is, in Galveston?"

The bartender chuckled. "No, I don't, but I'll tell you this, you aren't the first one to ask about her. She was a very good looking woman. We've had a lot of men come by, looking for her since she left."

"Have you heard from her?"

"Not directly, but one of the girls that used to work here heard from her. She said Chantal had come into a little money from somewhere, and was doing very well in Galveston."

"Is she now?"

"That's what they . . ." the bartender stopped in mid-sentence, then glared at someone who had just come in.

"Lundy, I told you not to come in here anymore. You're not welcome in Lafitte's."

"You ain't nothin' but the bartender, Eddie. You got no right to keep me out."

"No, but the owner of this place does. You're bad for business. The sailors know that you come in here to shanghai men, and they're afraid it might happen to them. We're losing customers."

"So what? It ain't like they won't be paid. The men I shanghai draw their wages same as any other sailor. Lots of 'em sign on for a second cruise."

"Maybe the men would like to choose the ship they serve on," Cade said. "Or maybe they don't want to go to sea at all."

Lundy looked at Cade, obviously irritated at the intrusion into his conversation with Eddie.

"What gives you the right to butt in to a private conversation?" Lundy asked.

"I'm one of the men you shanghaied," Cade said. "That means this particular conversation isn't all that private."

Lundy stuck his hand into his jacket pocket, and when it came out, it was clutching a Derringer pistol.

Cade was holding the heavy mug of beer by its handle, and he smashed it into Lundy's face before the contractor could thumb back the hammer. Lundy went down with a deep cut on his face, bleeding profusely.

Bending over, Cade picked up the little pistol, broke it down, unloaded it, then dropped it into a half-full spittoon.

"Give me a glass of whiskey and a clean towel," Cade said. When Eddie responded, Cade poured the whiskey on the cut on Lundy's face.

"Ow! What the hell are you doing, you son of a bitch?"

"Trying to keep the wound from putrefying, though I have no idea why."

Holding the towel over his cut, Lundy stood.

"Get out of here, Lundy. Get out of here now, and don't come back," Eddie ordered.

"Give me my pistol back," Lundy said to Cade.

Cade pointed to the half-filled spittoon. "I dropped it in there."

Lundy glared at Cade and Eddy, then, leaving his pistol un-retrieved and holding the towel over his wound, he left the bar.

"Hey!" one of the customers called. "Did you see that? That feller at the bar just knocked Lundy on his ass!"

The others cheered and applauded.

"Mister, let us buy you a drink!" the sailor offered.

"Well, I will take another beer," Cade said. "Somehow I seem to have spilled the one I had."

The steamship CRESCENT, with Captain J. Wilson as its master, was a four hundred ton vessel with a walking beam steam engine that turned side wheels. Part of Morgan Shipping Company's service between New Orleans and Galveston, it followed the coast line, never getting out of sight of land. It made the trip in two and a half days, dropping anchor at two-thirty in the afternoon on Thursday, the 21st of March.

Leaving the docks, Cade found himself on The Strand, a busy street filled with wagon traffic and, it seemed, more horses than people. Most of the men, he noticed, were wearing denim trousers tucked down into boots the tops of which came halfway up their calves. They wore colorful cotton shirts: red, blue, orange or yellow, and high-crown, wide-brim hats.

He decided then that one of the first things he was going to have to do was dress accordingly; otherwise he would stand out like a sore thumb. He had no particular plan in mind beyond finding Chantal and seeing if he would be able to recover any money, but he thought it would be better if he could blend in with the others.

He fought against the urge to buy new clothes right now though, thinking it would be best to study the town and its citizens for a while.

What better place to contemplate that, he asked himself, than a bar? And when it came to bars, he certainly had a broad choice. From where he was standing he could see half a dozen bars, though they seemed to refer to themselves as saloons. They were buildings with false fronts, across which the names were painted in brightly colored letters: Gem, Age, Texas King, Anchor, Stirrup and Saddle, and Cow Palace.

Because the money he had was the result of diamonds he had gathered in South America, he decided the Gem would be an appropriate choice, so he stepped inside, pushing through swinging, half-doors. Just inside he stopped and looked back at the doors. There didn't appear to be any doors other than those swinging panels, and while it did seem to facilitate the entry and exit, he couldn't help but wonder how they locked the place up at night.

Cade stepped up to the bar. The bartender, sporting a full, handlebar moustache, stepped up to him.

"Yes, sir, what'll it be?"

"Beer," Cade said.

"I'll be damn. We thought you were dead. Everyone in the 33rd Tennessee thought you were dead. You are Sergeant McCall, aren't you?"

When Cade turned toward the speaker, he saw a thin, wiry man with a light brown stubble on his chin. He was dressed exactly as all the men Cade had seen in the street, and, like many of those men, he was wearing a belt with a holstered pistol.

"Jeter Willis," Cade said with a big smile. "I haven't seen you since Franklin."

"No, I reckon not. And the last time I seen you, you was lyin' dead right in front of the cotton gin."

Cade chuckled. "I was lying there, all right, but I wasn't dead."

"Well I sure as hell thought you was, 'n ever' one else did too. Come on, Sergeant, bring your beer over to the table," Jeter said. "We've got a lot of catchin' up to do."

"I expect we do. And we can start with me no longer being a sergeant. The name is Cade."

"You just got off the boat, didn't you?" Jeter asked.

"Is it that obvious?"

Jeter laughed. "Well, if you had a sign hanging around your neck it might be a little more obvious."

"What are you doing here in Texas?" Cade asked.

"I mostly grow'd up in Texas. I might have wound up in the 33rd Tennessee, but I got there with General Hood's Division, and, like me, Hood was from Texas."

"Oh, yes," Cade said. "I had forgotten that."

"How is it you can be walkin' aroun' here like this, seein' as you was kilt at Franklin?"

"I wasn't killed at Franklin."

"Yeah, that's what you keep tellin' me." Jeter reached up and pinched Cade on the cheek.

"Ouch!"

"I reckon you're tellin' the truth all right," Jeter said. "I ain't never heard of no ghost you could pinch."

"Pinch me again and I'll knock you on your scrawny ass," Cade said with a laugh.

"I ain't goin' to do it no more now that I know you ain't dead."

Long Road to Abilene

16

FOR THE NEXT HOUR the men caught each other up on the last two years, with Cade telling about Pogue Elliot dying in the Yankee prison at Camp Douglas. He said nothing about his brother marrying Melinda, because even, after all this time, it wasn't something he wanted to talk about. He did tell about his adventures in South America, though he left out the part about being shanghaied, because he found that too embarrassing.

"I been right here in Galveston ever since I been back," Jeter said. "I drove a freight wagon some, rode shotgun on a stagecoach some, hell I even deputied a bit, but mostly what I've been doin' is punchin' cows at a couple near-by ranches."

"Punching cows? I'm not sure what that even means," Cade said.

Jeter laughed. "You're in Texas, and you don't know what punchin' cows means? You've got a lot to learn, 'n I reckon I'm goin' to have to be the one that learns you. Let me ask you this. You got 'ny money? The reason I ask is 'cause if you don't, I'll lend you some, on account of the first thing we have to do is get you out o' them Eastern duds 'n into some Texas clothes."

"I appreciate the offer of the loan, but I have some money left from my voyage to South America. And I was thinking about getting some different clothes, but I figured I'd have a beer first."

"All right, finish your beer 'n I'll go with you," Jeter said. "Lord knows you won't be able to buy 'em yourself, 'cause you won't have no idea in hell what to buy."

Cade didn't believe he had ever seen a store quite like Blum's, not even in Memphis or New Orleans. Here, less than one third of the inventory was given over to the type of clothing he was used to, the knee-length frock coats, shirts of patterned fabric, neckties and bowler hats. Those clothes were hanging on racks near the wall, almost as if Mel Blum had put them in his store as an afterthought.

The clothes that made up two thirds of his inventory were stacked up on long tables. The pants were separated by size and by denim or canvas. The shirts gave Cade a little more opportunity to express some personal preference, as they were separated by size, color, and style. Some of the shirts had a double-breasted panel, while the others had a single row of buttons.

"You think these pants will fit you?" Jeter asked, holding up a pair of brown canvas trousers.

Cade held them against his waist, then nodded. "Yeah, they'll fit."

"Better get two pair."

Cade reached for a pair of blue denims, and Jeter held his hand out. "You don't want those," he said. "Them's for farmin' or workin' in a mine. For cowboyin', you need the canvas."

When Cade left the store half an hour later, he was wearing new trousers, boots, and a yellow shirt. Carrying the rest of his purchases, as well as the clothes he had started the day with in a brown paper package, wrapped by the store, he followed Jeter out onto The Strand.

"Next thing we have to do is get you a rifle, pistol, and holster," Jeter suggested.

"Yes, I noticed that nearly everyone, including you, seems to be wearing a pistol."

"There," Jeter said, pointing to a store. The sign, painted in an arch across the front window read: GUNS, HOLSTERS, AMMUNITION.

The proprietor of the store was a small, bald-headed man who looked to be in his late forties or early fifties. He was wearing wire-rim glasses.

"What can I do for you gentlemen?" he asked, greeting the two men.

"My friend, here, needs to be outfitted," Jeter said.

"I won't need your help for this," Cade said.

"I reckon not," Jeter replied. "I recall that you was real good with guns in the army."

Cade picked up a Colt, double action, .45 caliber pistol. "I'll take this," he said. He reached for a Henry repeating rifle, exactly like the one he had used on the monitor, to repel boarders. "And this," he added.

"Have you got a room?" Jeter asked when they left the gun store a bit later. Cade, like Jeter and nearly every other man he saw, was now wearing his pistol in a holster.

"No, I just got off the boat, remember?" Cade replied with a broad smile.

"I'm staying in Mrs. Barrington's Boarding House," Jeter said. "I know she's got an extry room 'cause Dawkins signed on as an able bodied seaman to the OCEAN SPRAY, a couple of days ago, 'n Mrs. Barrington ain't put nobody else in it."

"What about that place?" Cade asked, pointing to a large, two-story white house with a red roof and red shutters. A wide, deep porch spread across the front of the house, and it was furnished with at least a dozen rocking chairs, some of them occupied. A sign on the well-kept lawn read: ARABELLA'S RED HOUSE.

"That's too high-falutin' for the likes of us," Jeter said. "Mostly it's just ship's captains, or rich cattlemen who stay there when they come into town. I'll say this, though . . . the woman that runs it, Arabella Dupree? She is one fine looking woman."

"Married?"

"I think she might be widdered, 'cause when she first come here she was a' wearin' widder's weeds. She didn' wear 'em all that long, 'n truth is, she looks a whole heap better without 'em. I reckon she figgered that since most of them that stays with her is men, it would be better for business if she didn't wear black all the time."

Jeter helped Cade get checked in at the boarding house, and once he got his room, Cade put away his extra clothes and the rifle.

"Tell me, Jeter, in your time here, have you run across a woman by the name of Chantal?"

"Chantal?" Jeter shook his head. "No, don't know as I've heard that name. Who is she?"

"I . . . uh, met her in New Orleans, but I heard that she's moved here."

"Pretty girl, is she?"

"Yes, so pretty in fact that, if she has come here, she'll most likely be working in a bar."

Jeter smiled. "Ah, so Chantal is THAT kind of a girl, is she?"

"Very much so."

"Wait a minute, what are you a' lookin' for a girl like that for, anyhow? I though you was all fired ready to marry up with Corporal Waters' sister, wasn't you?"

"It didn't work out," Cade said without any further explanation.

"So, are you plannin' on tryin' to find this Chantal?"

"Yes."

"All right, I'll tell you what. On account of because me 'n you is such good friends, I'd be willin' to go into ever' saloon they is in Galveston with you, 'n we'll just check out ever' one o' the little darlin's that's pushin' drinks. If this Chantal of yours is in town, we'll find her."

"She's not my Chantal," Cade replied, quickly.

"Then does that mean that if we find her, I can have her?"

Cade laughed. "Careful what you ask for, you may wind up with more than you bargained for."

"We'll try the Gem first," Jeter suggested. "I know they ain't no one by the name of Chantal that works there, on account of it bein' my favorite saloon 'n all, it's where I go the most 'n if they was a Chantal there, I would know her. But, I've made some friends there so we can ask around. Maybe someone there would have heard of her, especially one of the girls."

Once again, Cade was curious about the swinging doors as they stepped into the Gem.

"What are you lookin' at?" Jeter asked, when he saw Cade studying the entryway.

"I don't see any doors, except for these," Cade said. "How do they secure this place when it is closed?"

"Hell, that's easy," Jeter answered with a chuckle. "They don't need no solid doors, on account of this place ain't never closed."

Jeter called out to one of the bar girls. "Hey, Lucy, come here, I want you to meet a friend of mine."

Lucy was dressed to flaunt all her assets. She also had long, red hair.

"Oh," she said, flashing a broad smile when she approached. "A red head, just like me."

"His hair ain't red like yours. His hair ain't hardly red a' tall," Jeter said.

"Well, honey, I use a bottle to make my hair even redder, I don't expect this gentleman does," Lucy said.

"He wants to ask you somethin'," Jeter said.

"Well, we don't have to rush this," Cade said, returning Lucy's smile. "Let's have a beer."

Lucy called another girl over, and the two joined Cade and Jeter. Lucy, as women invariably did, ran her finger over the hook-like scar on Cade's forehead.

"Jeter said you wanted to ask me something?" Lucy asked after a few minutes.

"Yes. I'm looking for a woman."

Lucy's smile broadened. "Well, honey, you've found one."

"No," Cade said. "I mean a specific woman. I knew her in New Orleans, but I heard she has moved here."

"Darlin', Galveston is a big place," Maude, the other girl said. "And Lucy 'n me don't exactly mix with the fine ladies of the town."

"Neither would the woman I'm looking for," Cade said.

"What's her name?" Lucy asked.

"I only know her first name."

"One name is all any of us have," Maude said with a laugh.

"Her name is Chantal. She's Cajun."

The two women looked at each other for a moment, then Lucy spoke.

"I don't think either one of us have ever heard of her."

None of the other girls in the Gem had heard of her either, and the search in the Age, Texas King, and Cow Palace proved just as unproductive.

"Let's try the Anchor," Cade suggested.

"We ain't goin' to find 'er there, neither," Jeter said. "The Anchor is mostly for sailors, there ain't hardly no cowboys that ever goes there."

"I met her in a sailors' bar," Cade said.

"Yeah, that's right, you was a sailor for a bit, wasn't you?"

Cade didn't tell Jeter that he had been shanghaied in that sailors' bar, and that Chantal was the one who had set it up. If she was still in that business, the Anchor would be the most logical place for her.

Their visit to the Anchor proved to be as fruitless as had been all the others.

From the Anchor, they went to the Stirrup and Saddle, the sixth saloon they had visited. They asked about Chantal here as well, but got the same negative response. The bar girls, seeing no immediate future in spending time with the two men, moved on to more productive ground, leaving Cade and Jeter alone at a table.

Jeter had drunk a beer in every saloon they had visited, but Cade had switched to coffee after the second saloon, and was drinking coffee now.

"Maybe she didn't actual come to Galveston," Jeter suggested. "Or maybe she did come here, only she left to go somewhere else."

"I think you may be right," Cade conceded. "I knew that finding her would be a long shot, but I thought I would at least give it a try."

"She must 'a been some woman for you to come over here just to find her."

Cade smiled. "How do you know I didn't come over here to just look up an old friend from the war?"

"I have to confess that when I first seen you over at the Gem, I thought you was a haint," Jeter said. "I mean, seein' as I seen you layin' there dead with all the others that had been kilt. Only here you are, 'n you ain't no haint, you're real."

"You aren't going to pinch me again, are you, Jeter?"

"No, I ain't goin' to pinch you again," Jeter replied with a little laugh.

"What do you plan on doin' now?" Jeter asked. "I mean, seein' as you come here to find Chantal, 'n didn' find her."

"I don't know, I hadn't given it that much thought."

"Why don't you come on a cow hunt with me 'n Johnny Lattigo?"

"A cow hunt?"

"Yeah, me 'n Johnny's got us a plan. They's thousands of cows that don't belong to nobody that's just wanderin' around over in Jackson and Lavaca counties."

"What do you mean, they don't belong to anybody?"

"They're called mavericks. Long time ago some bulls 'n cows escaped, 'n since then they's thousands of cows that's been borned. All we got to do is round 'em up, then take 'em up to Kansas. We can get thirty dollars a head for 'em up there. Why, say we was to round up seven hunnert 'n fifty cows, that'd be fifteen thousand dollars. That would give us enough money to hire maybe three or four drovers to help us drive the cows on up to Abilene, 'n that's where we'd sell 'em. Even with all the expenses paid, me 'n you 'n Lattigo would more 'n likely wind up with better 'n four thousand dollars apiece."

"You make that sound pretty easy," Cade said.

"Now, don't get me wrong, there ain't nothin' a' tall easy about it. First of all, roundin' up the cows ain't goin' to be easy. 'N the young bulls is all goin' to have to be castrated, then we're goin' to have to brand 'em all, so's folks will know their ours."

"You said castrate the young bulls, what about the old bulls?"

Jeter laughed again, and shook his head. "Lord, do you have a lot to learn. Well, here's your first lesson. You don't go messin' with no full grow'd bulls, 'n you for sure don't try 'n castrate one. Not unless you want one o' them horns stuck clear through you."

"All right, when do we start?"

"Lattigo's drivin' for the stage company right now, 'n he just took his last run to Houston. He'll get back tonight, 'n we'll start out tomorrow. That is, soon as we can get you a horse 'n saddle."

"I'll be ready."

"Listen, seein' as this is goin' to be our last night in town for a while, what do you say we get us a couple of women and do it up right?"

"I'd rather not, but you go ahead," Cade said.

"Wait a minute. You ain't still goin' to be a' lookin' for Chantal, are you? 'Cause I think we've done show'd that she ain't nowhere about in Galveston."

Cade chuckled. "No, I've given up looking for her. I think I'll just get a good dinner and go back to my room. All this cattle business is new to me, and I need to get myself ready for it."

"Fine, you do that. But just don't go thinkin' yourself out of it. 'Cause if you do, it'll be a big mistake."

"You don't have to worry about that. I'm actually looking forward to it now."

Cade was on Market Street when he saw the disturbance between a well-dressed young woman and a rather large, overbearing man.

"I told you when I seen you that if you didn't give me twenty dollars a week, I was goin' to tell what I know about you," the man said in a gutteral voice. "Well, you ain't paid me nothin' in the last three weeks, so I want the money now."

"Please, sir, I don't have that kind of money."

"Then why don't I take it out in a little trade?" the man said. "You ain't worth sixty dollars, so it'll take quite a few visits for you to catch up."

As the man reached for her, he tore the sleeve from her dress. The woman screamed.

"Back away from her, you son of a bitch!" Cade said, and even as he spoke the words, he pulled the man away from the woman then spun him around.

Angrily, the man swung at Cade, but Cade had anticipated it, and he ducked under the swing, then counterpunched, hitting the man on the chin. The bully went down.

"Are you all right, Miz Arabella?" another man asked, coming quickly to the scene. This man was wearing a star on his shirt.

"Oh, that awful man!" Arabella said.

"I'll kill you, you son of a bitch!"

The angry shout came from the man Cade had just knocked down.

"Cade, look out, he has a gun!" Arabella screamed in warning.

Whirling back toward the man on the ground, Cade saw that the man had drawn his pistol, and was pointing it at him. Thinking instinctively, Cade kicked the man in the head as hard as he could. The kick was brutally effective as blood and brain matter erupted from the side of the man's head.

Quickly, Cade dropped to one knee to examine him, but no examination was necessary.

"You killed him, Mister," the man with the badge said, stating the obvious.

Cade looked up to plead his case, but what the lawman said next indicated that no such plea was necessary.

"You really had no choice, it was clearly self-defense. Don't worry, nothin' will come from it, I'll take care of it."

"Thanks," Cade said.

17

THE MAN WITH THE BADGE extended his hand. "I'm Deputy Miller. This lady is Miz Arabella Dupree. I reckon we owe you our lives."

"Not necessarily. It looked to me like I was the one he was about to shoot."

"He wouldn't have stopped there," the deputy said.

During the exchange of words with the deputy, Cade never took his eyes away from the woman who had just been introduced to him as Arabella Dupree.

"Deputy Miller is right," Arabella said. "Mr. Jensen may well have killed us. But even so, I owe you my thanks for coming to my rescue as you did."

"Yeah, I saw Jensen grabbin' at you from down at the corner," Deputy Miller said. "But before I could get to you, this man stepped in. What did Jensen want with you, Miz Arabella? Why was he grabbing at you like that?"

"He . . . had done some work for me at the Red House, and he thought I owed him money. Believe me, I owed him nothing."

The deputy looked again toward Cade. "What is your name, anyway?"

For a brief second, Cade thought of giving a false name just as he had when he was taken onto the FREMAD. But the deputy's response indicated that there would be no trouble as a result of what had just happened.

"The name is McCall. Cade McCall."

"Cade, that's right. Miz Arabella did call you Cade, didn't she?"

"Yes, she did," Cade said pointedly, continuing to stare at Arabella. He had to give her credit, she made no effort to look away.

"Listen, Mr. McCall. Would you be so kind as to walk Miz Arabella back to her place? I don't think she needs to stay here while Jensen's lyin' there like that." He nodded toward the body. "I'll get the undertaker to come take care of him."

"I don't need anyone to walk me back," Arabella said.

"Oh, it's all right, I'll be glad to do it," Cade said pointedly.

By now other people were beginning to gather at the grizzly scene so when Cade indicated they should leave, Arabella didn't protest.

They were half a block away before Cade spoke.

"What happened to your phony French accent?"

"The accent FRANCAIS was real, Monsieur," she said with a strong accent. "It is my Texas accent that is phony," she added, affecting a flat, Texas twang.

"And the name, Chantal? Was it real as well?"

"Arabella Dupree is my real name."

"You called me Cade. How did you know my name?"

"You told me your name."

"Yes, but of all the men you must have . . . uh . . . known, how is it that you remembered me?"

"It was easy. You are red headed, you have an interesting scar on your forehead, and you were the last man I arranged for Lundy to shanghai."

"You forgot something."

"Yes. You were the only man I ever stole fourteen hundred and twenty- seven dollars from," Arabella added.

By now they had reached the Red House. "I came here right after you left, and used the money to buy the Red House. This is my place now," she said, taking it in with a wave of her hand.

"Our place," Cade corrected

There was an elegant restaurant as part of the Red House. There were also private dining rooms and it was to one of those rooms that Arabella had taken Cade.

"I want to thank you again for coming to my rescue," Arabella said after they were seated.

"What did he really want with you? I'm sure it wasn't to be paid for some work he had done."

"He knew about my background. I've established a legitimate name for myself here, and he threatened to tell everyone of my unsavory past. I gave him some money thinking it would placate him, but it didn't. He kept coming back for more."

"Are you really a widow?"

Arabella smiled. "You really have investigated me, haven't you? No, I've never been married, but I thought coming here as a widow would keep people from asking questions."

"You mean like I'm doing now?"

"No. You have every right to ask questions, especially given our past relationship."

That's what you call our two times together? It was a relationship?"

"I know how angry you must be with me."

"Angry? Now, why should I be angry? All you did was steal fifteen hundred dollars from me."

"Fourteen hundred and twenty – seven dollars," Arabella corrected.

"But the worst thing you did was arrange for me to be shanghaied. That took eighteen months of my life away from me and nearly got me killed by putting me in the middle of a war in South America. Believe me, I had already been in one war, I didn't need to be in another one."

"Sailors are shanghaied all the time. Some of them expect it as a way of getting their next berth. I thought you would be more angry about the money I took, than arranging for you to be shanghaied."

"Why? I will never get those eighteen months back. I can always get the money back. In this case, it was just an investment."

"Investment? Yes, you did say our place, didn't you?" Arabella replied.

"I did." Cade smiled. "And our place seems to be doing quite well."

"Cade, you don't intend to, uh, do anything that would embarrass me, do you? Right now I have a position in Galveston society, I belong to at least three women's clubs, but if information about my past would get out somehow, my reputation, and OUR investment would come crashing down." Arabella emphasized the word, 'our'.

"Your secret is safe with me," Cade said.

"How do you want to handle your investment?"

"I want you to put half of your profits into a box, each month. When that box has fourteen hundred and twenty – seven dollars in it, give it to me, and I'll make no further claim."

Arabella smiled, broadly, and reached across the table to put her hand on Cade's arm. "You are being most gracious about this, Monsieur," she said in the heaviest French accent. "After dinner, why don't we take a bottle of Champagne to my apartment and celebrate?"

"Oh, no," Cade said, shaking his head. "I remember what happened the last time I drank Champagne with you and, like New Orleans, Galveston is on the water."

"I'll let you open the bottle, and I'll drink it first," Arabella said, laughing.

* * *

Johnny Lattigo was at least twenty years older than either Cade or Jeter. His gray hair was kept relatively short, and his gray moustache covered his mouth. His eyes were a light blue, and, like Cade, he had a scar on his face, a dark red lightning flash down his left cheek.

"The more we bring in, the lower our cut," Lattigo complained.

"If I'm a part of it, he's a part of it," Jeter said. "And if that don't work for you, me 'n him will go off 'n start our own cow hunt."

"No, no, now, there ain' no need for you to go off 'n be doin' 'nything like that. I was just commentin' is all, I wasn't actual complainin'."

"The first thing we've got to do is get ourselves outfitted," Jeter said.

"What does that take?" Cade asked.

"At least three horses, a good saddle, ropes, and chaps," Lattigo said.

"And a skillet, a dutch oven, a coffee pot, a cup 'n a tin plate," Jeter added.

"Me 'n Jeter been savin' our money to get ready for this," Lattigo said to Cade. "You got enough to outfit yourself, or are we goin' to have to make you a loan?"

"How much will it all cost?" Cade asked.

"It'll come to about two hundred and fifty dollars," Jeter said.

Cade nodded. "I've got enough."

"Damn, sailorin' must 'a paid real good," Jeter said.

"I managed to pick up a little extra money while I was in South America," Cade said.

They spent the next two days putting together what they would need for their adventure. Once they were completely outfitted, they headed west toward Jackson County.

* * *

"Does somebody live here?" Cade asked, when the three men stopped in front of a small, log cabin on the bank of the Navidad River.

"Yeah, we do, seein' as we're the first ones here," Jeter answered with a smile. "But as you can see, there ain't nothin' in it, 'n the door and winders is all open."

"I wonder who built it."

"There don't nobody really know who it was that actual built it, but it's got a corral we can use for the casteratin' 'n brandin', 'n a good pasture with enough grass 'n water to keep the cows content 'till we can start north with 'em," Lattigo said. "I was here three years ago with some others, 'n we used it then. Now it belongs to whoever is here first."

"And that's us," Jeter said.

"I figure, with the three of us, we should be able to round up about twenty-five to fifty a day. Say we can only get twenty-five a day, within a month we'll have seven hunnert 'n fifty cut 'n our brand, then we'll take 'em up to Abilene 'n sell 'em there."

The corral fencing had fallen down in a dozen or more places, and for the first few days the only thing they did was make the repairs. Then came the first day of the actual roundup.

Cade learned that the cattle tended to stay in the brush during the day time, wandering out only at night. Because of that, the best time for catching the cows was from two hours before sunrise, until the sun actually rose. They also had luck catching them on the nights when the moon was bright enough for them to see.

It didn't take Cade long to learn how to rope a cow. Jeter showed him that all he had to do was ride up close enough to one with a loop that was wide enough, and it was a matter of just dropping it over their heads . . . making sure that he cleared the horns then wrapping the rope around the saddle horn a few times so the horse would be the one to take up the initial shock. Then, most of the time, they could lead the cow on in to the corral.

The three men came up with a brand, and because they wanted one that would be easy to apply they settled on IIIX. They were able to do that with a branding iron that consisted of only one vertical bar, crossing it to make the X.

"Were you in the war, Lattigo?" Cade asked one night as the three men were having their supper.

"Yeah," Lattigo said. "But I didn' wear the same color you two boys wore."

"As far as I'm concerned, now, it doesn't matter what uniform we wore. We all faced the same dangers, we all saw friends killed, Yank or Reb," Cade said.

"You got that right."

"And a lot of us have the scars to prove it," Cade continued, putting his finger on his scar.

"Yeah, only, I didn't get this scar in the war," Lattigo said.

"Oh?"

"I run into a Mex who needed a horse 'n he thought I might give him mine, 'n we had a little scuffle over it." Lattigo put his finger over his own scar, which was longer, and more disfiguring that Cade's. "He left me permanently scarred, 'n I left him permanently dead," he added.

A couple of weeks after that discussion they were in the process of castrating and branding one day, when two men rode up.

"You know them fellers, Lattigo?" Jeter asked, just as a freshly branded cow got up and started quickly toward the other side of the corral.

Lattigo took his hat off, and brushed a fall of hair from his forehead. "Yeah," he said. "I know 'em."

When Lattigo started toward the fence, Cade and Jeter followed.

"What brings you out here, Harris?" Lattigo asked.

"Now is that any way to treat an old friend?" Harris replied with a greasy smile.

"We rode for the Diamond T brand, but I never thought of us as particular friends. What brings you out here?"

"To be honest, me 'n a few more boys was plannin' on doin' the same thing you're doin'."

"Go ahead, there's a lot more cows out here than we'll be able to collect."

"Yeah, well, the thing is, we was plannin' on usin' this cabin 'n corral."

"You're goin' to have to find your own place. We was here first, 'n we proved it up by repairin' the fence."

"Do you care if we take a look at some of your cows, just to see what kind of mavericks is out here?"

"Be my guest," Lattigo replied. "But climb the fence, don't open the gate. Some of 'em is still pretty spooked, 'n I don't want to have to go roundin' 'em up again."

Harris handed his reins to the rider who had come out with him, then climbed the fence and walked through the corral, checking the cattle.

"How many more you plannin' on gatherin'?" Harris asked.

"We've got nearly five hundred now," Lattigo said. "We're thinking about another two hundred fifty."

"What you plannin' on doin' with 'em?"

"We're goin' to drive 'em up to Abilene."

"Linus Puckett will take 'em all off your hands right now, for ten dollars a head."

"Why should we sell to the LP for ten dollars, when we can sell 'em in Abilene for thirty dollars?"

"You have to get 'em there first. Puckett is taking a big herd up to Kansas, he'll put your cows in with his, 'n you won't have to worry about takin' 'em up."

"No thanks."

Lattigo was unusually quiet over supper that night.

"What is it, Lattigo?" Jeter asked. "You ain't spoke more 'n half a dozen words since them boys left this afternoon."

"Harris is up to no good," Lattigo said.

"What do you mean?"

"I don't know what he has in mind, but I know the son of a bitch, 'n he ain't worth the gunpowder it would take to blow his nose. He mentioned that we rode for the Diamond T? He cut some cows out for 'is own. I should 'a told Mr. Taylor then, but I didn't, 'n when Taylor found out I know'd about it 'n didn't tell 'im, he fired me. 'N truth to tell, he had ever' right to fire me. No, sir, Harris has got somethin' planned, 'n I don't have 'ny idea what it is."

"Five hundred and seventy-five wearing our brand," Cade said proudly the next day, after having counted all the cattle in the pasture.

"I'll go into Texana this afternoon and see if I can get a couple boys to make the drive with us."

"You ain't goin' to get no cowmen in Texana," Jeter said. "Hell, there ain't nobody there but sailors."

"There are a lot of sailors who haven't always been seamen," Cade said. "And a lot of those are not all that anxious to ship out again."

"Yeah," Jeter said with a grin. "I reckon you would know about somethin' like that, wouldn't you?"

"I'm sure we can find a couple of men we can use," Lattigo said. "And as soon as we get seven hundred fifty head put together, we'll start north."

"Lattigo?" Jeter said. There was a curious tone to his voice. "Looks like we got company."

Looking in the direction Jeter pointed, Cade saw at least six men riding toward them. He recognized one of them as Harris, the man who had visited them yesterday. Two of the approaching men were wearing stars on their vest.

"Who are all those men?" Jeter asked. "What are they doing here?"

"I don't know, but I don't like it. That's Sheriff Boskey." Lattigo walked out to them. "Harris, what is this? Why have you brought the sheriff out here?"

"I've come to collect my cows," Harris said.

"What do you mean, you've come to collect your cows? What are you talking about?"

"Tell 'im, Sheriff." Harris could barely control the grin on his face.

"Lattigo, are all these cows wearing the same brand? The IIIX?" the sheriff asked.

"Yes. They were mavericks, Sheriff. We rounded them up and branded them ourselves."

"With the IIIX brand?"

"Yes, I told you. That's our brand."

"No it ain't," Harris said. "It's my brand."

"What the hell are you talking about? What do you mean, that's your brand?"

"Mr. Harris is right, Lattigo. He has filed on the IIIX brand. There is no record that you boys have. That means every cow wearing that brand belongs to Eb Harris."

"You'll play hell gettin' these cows," Lattigo shouted. Hurrying back to the corral, he reached for his pistol which was in the holster hanging over the fence.

"Lattigo, no!" the sheriff shouted. "Don't you pull that gun!"

"You son of a bitch! You ain't gettin' our cows!"

By now the sheriff and two other men had already drawn their weapons and all three fired. Lattigo went down under a hail of bullets.

Jeter ran to his fallen friend.

"Get away from him!" the sheriff shouted. "Willis, get away from there. The two of you, stand aside!"

"You killed him," Cade said.

"You seen what happened. He was goin' for his gun, we didn't have no choice. Harris, get your cows, and let's get out of here."

"You can't do that!" Jeter said. "You can't just come in here 'n take our cattle like that."

"It's like I told you," the sheriff said. "Seein' as how you didn't file that brand with the county and Harris did, they're his cows." He held up a piece of paper. "I've got a court order from Judge Briggs, saying that. I'm sorry, boys. There's nothing I can do."

Cade and Jeter stood to one side as Harris, and the men he brought with him, drove the cows out of the pasture and across the plain. Flies were beginning to buzz around Lattigo's body.

Long Road to Abilene

18

COLONEL LINUS PUCKETT had a sixty thousand acre ranch that was bordered by the Navidad River to the east, and the Lavaca River to the west. He was a slender man with a receding hairline and bushy, white eyebrows, and he was called Colonel, because of his storied Texas history. During the war for Texas Independence he had been with Sam Houston at the Battle of San Jacinto. During the Mexican War he was with Zachary Taylor at the Battle of Buena Vista, and during the Civil War he had served as a Colonel with General John B. Hood from the Texas Brigade, all the way to the Army of Tennessee.

He had been at the Battle of Franklin.

"Who were you boys with?" Puckett asked when he learned that both Cade and Jeter had been at the same battle.

"General Stewart's Corps, General Cleburne's Division, Colonel Hill's Regiment, and Captain Hanner's company," Cade replied.

"Cade was a sergeant," Jeter added.

"Wars are won by the sergeants, not by the generals," Puckett said. "So, you two boys are looking to join the drive to Abilene, are you?"

"Yes, sir," Cade said.

"Any particular reason why you want to go? I ask this because I need to be one hundred percent confident in the loyalty of my riders to the brand."

"You'll have our loyalty, Colonel. Especially to the cows wearing the IIIX brand," Cade said.

Colonel Puckett' eyes narrowed. "The IIIX brand? Are you talking about the cows I bought from Eb Harris?"

"Yes."

"Why do you have a particular interest in them?"

Cade and Jeter told Colonel Puckett about rounding up the maverick cattle, branding them, and holding them in the corral they had repaired.

"We planned to start north as soon as we got seven hundred and fifty head," Cade said.

"Then Eb Harris stole our herd," Jeter said.

"Look here, boys, I . . ." Colonel Puckett started to say, but Cade held up his hand to stop him.

"Colonel, we've got no beef with you. What you did was perfectly legal. What Harris did was within the law as well. Legalized larceny, you might call it. It was our fault for not getting our brand registered."

"We wound up losing our herd, and Johnny Lattigo wound up gettin' hisself kilt," Jeter said.

"I'm sorry to hear that boys," Colonel Puckett said. "I knew nothing about all that. Harris told me that he and a couple of his friends had rounded up the cattle, and he showed me the certificate of brand registration to establish his ownership of the herd."

"It's like Cade said, Colonel, we ain't neither one of us blamin' you. Only now we're a' needin' work, 'n if you'll hire us, we'd like to go on the drive with you."

Colonel Puckett stroked his chin for a moment as he studied the two men who had come to ask for employment.

"I'll tell you what I will do. The IIIX cattle still have a little wild in them. As we make the drive north, I'd like to keep them somewhat separated from the rest of the herd because I don't want any of that wild rubbin' off onto my tame cows. If you two men will be personally responsible for them, I'll pay you two dollars and fifty cents a head for every IIIX cow we are able to get to market.

"I know that's a long way from the thirty dollars a head you were counting on."

Cade and Jeter glanced at each other and smiled.

"Colonel, you've got yourself a deal," Cade said, extending his hand. Jeter shook hands as well, and with that the two men became riders for the brand. In the broader sense they were riding for the LP brand, but now, specifically, they were riding for the IIIX.

"We'll make a common camp at night," Colonel Puckett said. "But during the day, keep your bunch about a quarter of a mile behind us. I want you close enough so we can keep in touch with each other, but far enough apart that the cows don't intermix. I'll give you Old Rudy as a lead steer. He's made this drive three or four times, he knows what to do, and the other cows will follow him. And, I'll give you one more rider, that'll give you one on each flank, and one to ride drag."

Getting the herd underway would require as much organization as mobilizing an army regiment. Colonel Puckett was quite comfortable with that, because command sat easily upon his shoulders. Counting Cade and Jeter, there would be eighteen drovers making the drive. He also had a chuck wagon and hoodlum wagon. The hoodlum wagon carried bedrolls, firewood, extra gear, and provided the cook with space to carry more food.

The cook's name was Rufus Slade. There was nothing about the cook's appearance that made him any different from anyone else until one looked in his eyes. His eyes were deep and cryptic, as if hiding a past he didn't want anyone to know about. Unlike many ranch and camp cooks, Rufus

Slade didn't talk much, and when he did talk he used as few words as necessary.

The driver of the hoodlum wagon was Ian Campbell. Ian, who was sixty years old, had come to America when he was in his mid-twenties. Some said it was to find a better life, some said it was because he had been jilted by a woman, and a few even suggested that Ian, who even in his sixties was still a big and powerful man, had killed someone with his bare hands.

The horse wrangler was Van Beecher. Van was only fourteen, too young to handle cattle, though he could manage the small herd of horses. Van was also the cook's assistant; he washed the dishes, took care of the camp gear, and gathered the wood for the evening fire when the entourage stopped for their noon meal. Van showed up at the LP Ranch when he was twelve years old, offering to work for food. He had run away from an orphanage, and though Colonel Puckett's first thought had been to take him back, he let the boy move into the bunkhouse with the other hands and his willingness to do anything asked of him made him a favorite of the cowboys. This was his second cattle drive.

Most of the horses Van looked after belonged to the brand, but Cade and Jeter had brought their own horses to the drive. After Lattigo was killed, Cade and Jeter had taken his horses, sold one and kept the other two. That gave them a personal string of four horses each, which were kept in the remuda with the others.

The LP herd, including the five hundred and seventy-five cows the colonel had bought from Harris, numbered just over four thousand, and on the day they were to begin the drive, Rufus had prepared an enormous breakfast for them: bacon, biscuits, gravy, scrambled eggs, and grits.

"Damn, Rufus, you goin' to feed us this good for the whole drive?" Boo Rollins asked. Rollins was the drover who would be with Cade and Jeter, working the IIIX cows.

"Better eat a lot," Lou Porter said. "I've been on a lot of these drives, 'n when the cook starts out with a breakfast like this, why we don't normally get nothin' else to eat for near a week."

"Porter you are as full of shit as a Christmas goose," one of the other drovers said, his comment met with good-natured laughter.

As soon as breakfast was over, the chuck wagon, hoodlum wagon, and the herd of horses started out. They would go ahead about seven or eight miles and find a good place for the nooning.

Although most cattle ranchers didn't do so, Colonel Puckett would be acting as his own trail boss, and with all the cattle in place, he stood in his stirrups and shouted the order.

"All right! Head 'em up, and move 'em out!"

Cade, Jeter, and Boo had already put some separation between the cows they would be moving and the rest of the herd, so they waited for about fifteen minutes before they started after the others.

For the first several days they pushed the cattle fairly hard to get them away from their customary ranges, and to make them too tired to run at night. After the first week the cattle settled down so that everything fell in place. The cattle started moving each morning, bawling and mooing in protest of leaving their comfortable ground, but quickly falling into the same relative position they had held in the herd on the day before. Cade recalled his time in the army, and he couldn't help but think of this operation, not as cows being prodded along, but as a division of infantry, each in his own place, following the orders of Colonel Puckett and the officers and non-commissioned officers over them.

The one thing Cade hadn't considered was what it would be like to sit a saddle for several hours per day. About ten days into the drive, they were making camp one night when Jeter noticed Cade limping around.

"Got a sore ass, do you?" Jeter teased.

"I have to confess that it has felt better."

"You just ain't spent that much time on a hurricane deck is all."

Cade laughed. "I know you're talking about a saddle, but to someone who has sailored a bit, the term hurricane deck has a different meaning. You're right though, I've never spent this much time in the saddle."

"Don't worry about it, sailor man," Porter said. "Before we get to Abilene, you'll have so many callouses on your ass that a mule could kick you 'n you'd just laugh at 'im."

"Like the man said, Porter, you're as full of shit as a Christmas goose," Cade teased.

The drive proceeded day in and day out without incident, progressing an average of fifteen miles per day.

"One thing we got to always be on the lookout for is a run," Jeter cautioned, continuing his self-imposed mission of "learnin'" Cade the cowboy business.

"A run?"

"Yeah, a stampede," Jeter said. "They's damn near anythin' that can set 'em a' runnin, a man's hat blowin' off, or somebody a' sneezin', or just any old thing. I oncet seen a stampede get started 'cause someone dropped his coffee cup. 'N it can happen with any herd, too. Cows that don't get upset by lightenin' 'n thunder on Monday, might start a' runnin' on Tuesday just on account of they don't like the song some drover is a' singin'."

Less than a week after Jeter had told Cade about stampedes, and just after the two herds were merged for the night, something, and nobody was sure what it was, spooked the cows and the stampede was on.

"Stampede! Stampede!" someone shouted, but the call wasn't necessary, the thunder of the cattle's hooves was all the alarm needed. The horses had been turned into the remuda for the night but saddles were quickly thrown on and every man mounted. The riders carried blankets, coats, shirts, towels, anything that could be waived, and so armed, they galloped out beyond the fleeing animals.

Cade felt his heart pounding in his chest, whether from fear or excitement, he didn't know. Riding at full gallop at night meant the horse could hit a hole, break his leg, and throw his rider. Not since the storm on board the FREMAD had he been so on edge to the attendant danger.

Although Jeter had talked about stampedes, he hadn't been clear on how they were to be handled, so Cade just followed the others and did as they did, getting ahead of the running cows. He knew they wouldn't be able to stop a herd of four thousand at full gallop, but he saw quickly that they weren't trying to stop the herd, they were just trying to turn them.

Gradually the front of this column began to react to the urging of the horsemen, and the herd was turned back onto itself by whooping and hollering cowboys who were firing pistols into the air.

This started the cattle into a large, circle of bellowing cows, surrounded by a cloud of choking dust that hung in the air, made somewhat iridescent by the bright, full moon. The milling was kept up until finally the cattle quit from exhaustion. Then, no longer running, they moved about, only to resume their self-appointed positions within the herd, which meant that the IIIX cows separated themselves from the others. When the herd was exactly where it started, they stood quietly as if nothing had happened.

After it was over a nose-count was taken, and they came up one man short.

"Where's Porter?" Colonel Puckett asked.

"Maybe he just ain't come back in yet," another answered.

"Yeah," another said. "He'll be back in soon."

Cade and the others, exhausted from their ordeal, crawled into their blankets for a welcome sleep.

Cade learned about Porter's fate at breakfast the next morning. The last relief of the nighthawks, who were in the saddle when the sun rose, saw him, or what was left of him. He had been thrown, knocked off, or had fallen from his horse during the stampede and the cattle, which had been forced to mill, had run over him time, and time again.

"What makes me feel bad," Boo said, "is that we done that to him. We just kept them cows a turnin', 'n all that time Porter was layin' on the ground under 'em, gettin' hisself runned over."

"We didn't know he was in there, 'n even if we had knowd, why there warn't nothin' we could 'a done about it," Jeter said. "We couldn't 'a rode in through all them cows when they was a' circlin' like that."

19

IT WAS JUST AFTER DARK and the moon full and bright. Two night-hawks were out watching over the herd, while the others were back at the camp, chatting quietly. Lou Porter was the subject of the conversation, and those who knew him, were telling stories about him.

"Me 'n Porter went to San Antone oncet," Jess Unger said. "Porter said he know'd someone there that could give us a good, easy job where we wouldn't have to do nothin' but sit on our ass 'n keep an eye on hosses that belonged to the stagecoach line. Onliest thing is, his friend warn't there no more, 'n we wound up muckin' out stables, which is about the hardest, 'n most stinkinest job a feller could get. One day he was fillin' buckets with hoss shit and passin' it up to me so's I could carry it off 'n get rid of it.

"'Porter, I thought you said me 'n you would be gettin' us a good job here,' I says to 'im.

"'You the one with the bad job. I got a good job here,' Porter says.

"'What do you mean you got a good job here?' I asks. 'We got the same job.'

"'No we don't' he says. 'You don't see me takin' shit from anyone, do you?'"

The others laughed, and that story about Porter was followed with still more stories about the cowboy they had lost, some funny, some poignant.

"It don't seem right, just leavin' 'im buried out here on the prairie like we're doin'," Van said.

"Hell, boy, you got 'ny idea how many folks there is that's buried out here like this?" Unger asked. "I wouldn't' be surprised if there wasn't near 'bout as many buried out on the plains like that, as there is buried in town cemeteries."

Cade, who had only recently met Porter, had nothing to add to the conversation, so he just sat there listening to the others, staring into the fire. He liked to see the flames nearest the wood just at the point where the blue turned to a flickering orange.

"Cade, is it true you was oncet a sailor?" Boo asked, when the conversation lagged.

Cade glanced toward Jeter.

"Don't get mad at me now, Cade, I told 'em, you was a sailor. Hell, I think that's real interestin'."

Cade nodded. "Yes, I was a sailor."

"Did you like sailorin'?" Unger asked.

Cade started to say no, then he thought of Bento, Willoughby, Pops, and Stumpy.

"I made some good friends," he said, without specifically answering Unger's question.

"Aye, 'twas sailing before the mast that brought me here from Scotland," Campbell said. "And no better friends can ye find but in the fo'c'sle."

"In the what?" Van asked.

"The fo'c'sle is where we slept," Cade said. "When we slept."

Campbell laughed. "Aye, that's surely a fact, lad, for an ordinary seaman finds but little time to sleep."

Rufus Slade had been squatting on his haunches, listening to the conversation without participating. After a few minutes he stood up, walked over to the chuck wagon, then returned, carrying a pan. The pan was filled with cookies, and he passed them out to the others.

"Damn!" Unger said. "Who knew this? Slade, you just like a mama to us poor cowboys."

"I'm not your mama," Rufus replied.

A few days later, Colonel Puckett halted the drive just outside of Ft. Worth This would be the last opportunity to restock the dwindling food supplies before going into "The Nations". Puckett also intended to check, by telegraph, on the current stock prices in Abilene. If it had fallen to less than twenty-five dollars a head, he would turn around and go back to the LP Ranch.

For the drovers, though, Ft. Worth would provide a much needed respite from the long drive. It also gave Cade the opportunity to send a letter to his brother. He had had no contact with him since sending him the money to save the farm. He thought it was about time to do so.

Dear Adam,

I am sure you are about as surprised to get this letter from me as you were when you learned that I was still alive. I am happy to report that I am still alive, and I am getting along fine. I hope you, Melinda, and the baby are doing well.

I have settled in Texas, and as of this writing I am in the employ of Colonel Linus Puckett, who is the owner of the LP Ranch in Jackson County, Texas. In this capacity I am taking part in a cattle drive, which means that I, along with seventeen other drovers are pushing a herd of four thousand cows up to Abilene, Kansas. Abilene is the closest point where we can put the cows on trains to be taken to meat markets in the East.

You may reply to me, care of LP Herd, Abilene, Kansas.

Sincerely, your brother,
Cade

"All right, boys, we'll stay here for two nights," the colonel said. "I don't want to leave the herd unguarded, so half of you can go in tonight, and half of you can go in tomorrow night. Work the schedule out among yourselves, but remember this when you go into town. The gamblers are crooked, the drinks will be watered, and the only thing the women want from you is your money. Enjoy yourselves, but keep that in mind and stay out of trouble."

Even though the IIIX herd no longer belonged to them, Cade and Jeter still had a proprietary interest in the cows. The two men flipped a coin, and winning the toss, Cade chose to go in the first night.

Rufus had actually gone into town earlier. He planned to buy everything he needed today, then have it taken out to the herd by supply wagon tomorrow.

Ft. Worth was a small town, with saloons and businesses spread out along Main Street. When Cade and the others got there, Van, who was the wrangler and knew all the horses, pointed to a horse that was tied up in front of one of the saloons.

"That's the horse Mr. Slade is riding," he said.

"He must 'a got all the buyin' done already," Unger said.

"You think maybe he got 'ny canned peaches or somethin' like that?" Boo asked. "I sure would like me some peaches."

The name of the saloon, Nippy Jones, was painted in red and gold letters across the high false front.

"Tell me, Van, have you ever been in a saloon?" Cade asked as the eight riders tied off their horses.

"No, sir. I 'mos did when we come through here last year, but Colonel Puckett, he wouldn't let me come into town by myself. 'N when he come in with me, he wouldn't let me go into a saloon. He said I could go into one this time as long as I stayed out of trouble."

"Ha! You ain't nothin' but a boy," Boo said. "What kind of trouble does Colonel Puckett think you'd be gettin' in to?"

"OCH, he is but a boy, is he? And would ye' be for tellin' me what ye' are if not a bairn yourself?" Campbell asked.

The others, including Van, laughed.

Nippy Jones Saloon, like the Gem and other saloons in Galveston, had batwing doors across the front opening. But it did have solid doors that were folded back against the wall.

Two of the bar girls came to greet them.

"Oh, what a handsome bunch of men!" one of the girls said, and she reached out to put her hand on Unger's shoulder.

"I want all you fellers to see which one this fine lady picked when she said we was all handsome," Unger said. "It's clear that she thinks I'm the most handsome."

"Unger, 'tis thinkin' I am, that not even yer own mither would call ye handsome," Campbell said.

"Oh, an accent," the girl said. "What kind of accent is that?"

"Why, 'tis no accent at all, lass, for 'tis the tongue of Scotland. To me, everyone else sounds funny."

"There's Mr. Slade at the bar," Van said, pointing to the cook.

"You fellers go ahead 'n join 'im," Slim, one of the other cowboys said. "I see him ever' day. While I'm in here, I'll be spendin' my time with the ladies."

"Me too," Lefty said.

"Well, then you two gentlemen just come with us and we'll have a fine time," said one of the two girls who had met them when they first came in.

There was a roulette wheel at one of the tables, and a game of faro at another. One of the cowboys headed for the roulette wheel, but Unger started toward the faro table.

"If you boys want to find me, I'll be bucking the tiger," Unger said.

Cade, Boo, Van and Campbell joined Rufus Slade at the bar. The bartender, wearing a white shirt with sleeve garters, greeted them.

"What will it be, gents?"

"'N would ye be for tellin' me, mon, if 'tis a good Scotch ye keep here, or will I have to satisfy my thirst with some swill that is nay fit for man nor beast?" Campbell asked.

Smiling, the bartender reached under the bar then brought up an unopened bottle and set it before him. "How is this for you, friend? It was distilled from the finest barley in Scotland and the mist of the moors, cured for twenty years in a barrel of charred white oak cut from Paisley forest itself."

Campbell smiled broadly. "OCH, 'tis a good mon ye be. 'N if ye would pour me a glass I'll be for visitin' a bit of heaven when it reaches m' tongue."

"Beer," Cade said, and Boo ordered the same.

"And you?" the bartender asked Van.

"I'll have a beer too."

"Mr. Slade, did you get 'ny canned peaches?" Boo asked.

"They take up too much room," Slade replied.

"Oh," Boo said, clearly disappointed.

"Get up!" a loud voice called. "You know that's my chair."

When Cade and the others looked toward the loud, angry voice they saw a slender man with a dark moustache and black eyes. Like most in the saloon, he was wearing a pistol, but his rig was different from the others. It was all in one piece, the holster hanging down from the belt by a wide leather strip.

"You wasn't here, Mr. Shardeen, so I didn't figure it was your chair," a man said, getting up quickly and stepping away from the table.

"That's my chair all the time whether I'm here or not. I'd better never see you, nor anybody else in it again."

"No, sir, no sir, you won't never see me in it again," the man replied in a frightened voice.

"Nell, get over here," Shardeen called.

"I'm with these gentleman now, honey," Nell replied. She was one of the two girls who had accompanied the two LP cowboys to the table. "I'll be over there as soon as we finish our drink."

"You'll get over here now," Shardeen demanded.

"I'm sorry, honey," Nell said. "I've got to go to him."

"No you don't," Lefty said. "Not 'til you've finished your drink, you don't."

"Lefty, leave it be," Slim said, putting his hand across the table onto Lefty's arm to keep him from doing anything foolish. "I don't have a good feelin' about him."

When Nell joined Shardeen at his table, there was a noticeable reduction of tension in the saloon. That's when Slade saw that Van had taken no more than a sip from his glass.

"You don't like beer?" Slade asked.

"No, sir, none too particular," Van replied.

"Maybe you'll like this." Rufus handed Van a small, brown sack.

"What's that?"

"Just somethin' I got for you. Look inside," Rufus said.

A big grin spread across Van's face when he opened the sack. "Horehound candy!" he said excitedly. He took out a drop and put it in his mouth.

"Oh," he said. "I wasn't bein' very mannerly." He held out the sack to the others, all of whom declined. That was when Unger joined them.

"How did it go with you bucking the tiger?" Boo asked.

"I figured I'd better quit while I still had enough money to buy myself a beer."

"You can have mine," Van said, sliding his glass toward Unger.

"Well, now, Van, that's very kind of you," Unger said. "But what will you drink?"

"I think I'll have myself a sarsaparilla."

"A sarsaparilla? Did I just hear somebody order a sarsaparilla?" The question was loud, and dripping with ridicule. The volume and tenor of the question stopped all other conversation. It had come from Shardeen.

"I like sarsaparilla," Van replied.

"What are you doin' here, boy?" The tone of this question was just as derisive.

"I'm with the others. We ride for the LP. We're takin' a herd up to Abilene."

"Are you now?"

Cade turned toward the loud talker, and though he glared at him, he didn't say anything, mindful of the colonel's admonition to stay out of trouble.

Shardeen continued with his harangue. "I know that when drovers is out on the trail for a long time without no women, it sometimes gets lonely for 'em. Are you their sweet young thing?"

"What? I don't understand what you mean," Van said, confused by the question.

"Honey, why don't you leave the boy alone?" Nell said. "He isn't bothering anyone." She forced a smile. "Besides, you asked me over here to join you. How do you think it makes me feel, if you don't pay any attention to me?"

"Why the hell should I care what a whore feels like?" Shardeen asked.

"You got no call treating me like that," Nell said.

"I'll treat anyone, any way I want, 'n there's nobody that can do a damn thing about it."

Shardeen, now aware that Cade was glaring at him, stood up and moved away from the table.

"What the hell are you looking at?" Shardeen asked.

"Mister, I don't know what put that wild hair up your ass, but I think we've had about enough of you," Cade said.

The belligerent man smiled. "Well now, I was wonderin' when you was goin' to step up and defend your sweet young thing."

"Stay out of this, Cade," Rufus said. "Van is the cook's helper, and since I'm the cook that makes the boy my responsibility. I'll take care of this fool."

Shardeen laughed out loud. "The cook? You're the cook, and you're going to take care of me?"

"Find yourself another saloon, and leave us be," Rufus said.

"Now hold on there," Shardeen said, lifting his hand toward Rufus. "I was about willin' to let all this go, but I'll be damn if I'll be given orders by some belly robber."

"If you want to live, you'll find another saloon," Rufus said.

Shardeen's eyes narrowed. "Mister, do you know who I am?"

"Yeah, I know who you are. You are Luke Shardeen, and you fancy yourself a gunfighter. I also know that you've put the notches on your gun by killing drunks, young boys and old men."

Shardeen smiled. "Funny you would say that, bein' as you're an old man. You want to be the next notch?"

"There won't be a next notch, Shardeen," Rufus said. "If you don't leave this saloon right now, I'll kill you."

Cade had followed the exchange first with concern, then with interest, and now with shock. He had been with Rufus Slade for a little over a month but he couldn't say that he actually knew him, because Rufus kept to himself so. The cook had said more words in the last minute than Cade had heard him say in the whole time he had known him.

From his time in the army, in the Camp Douglas prison camp, and on board the FREMAD, Cade had developed a keen sense of reading people and situations. Right now he knew that this particular situation was about to come to a head. And that same ability to read people told him that Rufus was a much greater threat than Shardeen could possibly know.

"What is your name, cook? I'm going to want to remember you," Shardeen said.

"The name is Slade. Rufus Slade."

"Rufus Slade? Wait a minute? Are you saying you are the one they call Ruthless Slade?" Shardeen asked, his entire demeanor changing from one of arrogant confidence to uncertain fear.

"It's not a name that I like, but I have been called that," Rufus replied.

Without another word, Shardeen's hand dipped to his pistol, and he had it out in flash, firing as soon as he brought the gun up. The bullet from his gun slammed into the bar between Cade and Rufus.

There was a second shot, so close after the first that there was barely a discernable space between the two. The second shot was fired by Rufus and he stood there holding a smoking gun in his hand as Shardeen, with an expression of total shock on his face, went down.

"I thought you were dead," the Ft. Worth city marshal said. "I heard that Ruthless Slade was killed three, maybe four years ago, down in San Antonio. Nobody has heard anything about you since then."

"I didn't want anyone to hear from me," Rufus said. "I put that life, and that name behind me. Until today."

"Yeah, well everyone in the saloon said that Shardeen drew first. And I don't mind tellin' you, if there was ever a son of a bitch that needed killin' Luke Shardeen is the one. There won't be any need for the law."

20

ONLY TWO MEN in the outfit had known of Rufus Slade's background as a gunfighter. Colonel Puckett had known, and so had Ian Campbell.

"There was a time when Mr. Slade sold his gun," Colonel Puckett told Cade and Jeter. "He didn't sell it to the highest bidder, you understand, he sold it to the people who he thought were on the right side of any dispute. He was a paladin, you might say."

"A paladin?" Jeter asked. Cade was unfamiliar with the word as well, so he was glad that Jeter had asked.

"The word comes from the time of King Charlemagne. In the battle of good versus evil, a paladin is a warrior for the good."

"And now he is just a cook," Jeter said.

"Just a cook, Mr. Willis? Do you think there is something ignoble about being a cook? Do you think he is a bad cook?"

"No, no, nothing like that," Jeter said quickly. "I think he's a real good cook. I ain't never et no better beef 'n dumplins than what Rufus makes."

"I understand Jeter's comment though," Cade said. "Why did Rufus give up being a paladin?"

"It happened in San Antonio. Three men had been paid to assassinate Rufus, and during the shootout, Rufus killed four."

"Four? But you said three," Jeter said.

"Yes. Once the gunfight started, Rufus's closest friend came out of the saloon, gun in hand, to help Rufus. Rufus reacted only to a man with a gun in his hand, and he shot him. He killed his best friend."

Cade thought about what Colonel Puckett had told him about Rufus Slade, and having seen him in action, he could well understand how he could have been a gun for hire. And yet the Rufus Slade that he saw after they left Ft. Worth was totally unchanged from the Rufus Slade of before. He was a cook who was dedicated to feeding his men, and as taciturn as he had ever been. Cade waited several days before he approached Rufus with his request.

"Would you teach me?" Cade asked.

"Now why do I think you aren't asking me to teach you how to make biscuits?" Rufus replied.

Cade chuckled. "You're right. I want you to teach me how to use a gun the way you do. I know there must be something other than just good reflexes and coordination to having a fast draw."

"A fast draw," Rufus said. It wasn't a question; it was a declarative sentence dripping with derision.

"Yes, I'm sure there must be some procedure that you can learn for a fast draw," Cade said, having missed the scorn in Rufus's comment.

"Did you notice, Mr. McCall, that Shardeen got his gun out, and fired before I did?"

"Well, yes, but that's because he started his draw before you did."

"The other man must always draw first. Otherwise you'll be committing murder. Here's your first lesson. It isn't who shoots first; it is who hits what he is shooting at first."

"Yes, I can see how that would be so."

"Why do you want to do this?"

"Because I have seen good and evil," Cade replied. "And I want to be an agent for good."

"You want to be an agent for good? Tell me, if you can, what is good about killing?" Rufus asked.

Cade paused for a moment before he replied.

"I was in the war, Mr. Slade. I have seen thousands of men killed, and I was one of those doing the killing. It wasn't good versus evil. I killed good men, husbands, fathers, and sons, all of whom were loved by someone. And I killed them for no other reason than that they were wearing a different uniform than I was. You ask me what is good about killing? I can tell you for certain, that there is nothing, absolutely nothing, good about killing."

Rufus nodded. "You have given me the right answer. All right, I'll teach you."

"Thanks."

Rufus shook his head. "Don't thank me, Cade. You are about to step through a door into something that will take control of you for the rest of your life. There will come a time when you will curse the day you ever heard of me."

Cade began putting into practice the techniques Rufus showed him. He recalled the first lesson:

"When you grab the gun, you want to get a good grip by coming down hard on the handle, wrapping your thumb around one side, 'n all the fingers but the trigger finger round the other side. Keep your trigger finger pointin' straight down, on the outside of your holster, and don't even touch the trigger 'till you got the gun up level, otherwise you might wind up shootin' yourself in the leg.

"And the other thing is, you don't aim at your target."

"If you don't aim, how do you hit the target?" Cade asked.

"You think where you want the bullet to go."

"Thinking" the bullet to the target seemed like a bizarre concept, but before long Cade was able to use this kinesthetic sense to draw his pistol and put his bullets on target quickly, and with unerring accuracy.

Three weeks after leaving Ft. Worth the herd was pushed across the Red River without the loss of a single cow. Crossing the river meant they were out of Texas, and now in "The Nations". There, they were met by a delegation of Indians. Though some of them were dressed in native garb, many were wearing clothes that were no different from the clothes worn by the drovers.

One of the Indians, wearing buckskin that was decorated with dyed porcupine quills, dismounted and walked toward them. He held up his hand, palm facing the cowboys.

"Hello, my friends," he said. "I am Jimmy Standing Deer of the Cherokee Nation."

"Hello, Chief Standing Deer. I am Colonel Linus Puckett."

"You have many cows," Standing Deer said.

"Yes."

"You are taking your cows to Kansas?"

"Yes."

Standing Deer nodded. "That is good. In Kansas you will get much money for your cows."

"That's the idea," Colonel Puckett said.

"How many cows do you have?"

"A little over four thousand head."

"When your four thousand cows cross our land, they will eat our grass and they will drink our water. And when you want meat for your men, you will kill our deer and our rabbits and our birds. Is this right?"

"I suppose you could put it that way," Colonel Puckett said.

Standing Deer nodded. "Good, that is good. We will say one thousand dollars."

"One thousand dollars?"

"You must pay a toll of twenty-five cents for every cow that crosses our land."

"Last year it was only fifteen cents per head."

"Yes," Standing Deer said. "But last year the brokers in Abilene were paying only twenty-five dollars per head. Today they are paying thirty dollars per head. It is more money for all of us."

Colonel Puckett laughed. "Thanks for the latest market report, Chief. I'll pay your toll."

"Good, that is good," Standing Deer said. "We are friends, Colonel Puckett. And as friends, we will eat together. Tell your cook he can rest. Our women have prepared turkey, corn, beans, and squash."

It was a well-fed group of drovers who told the Indians goodbye.

Eighty-two days after Cade and the others started the herd north from the LP ranch, they reached the bedding ground, one mile south of Abilene.

"You ain't never seen nothin' like Abilene Town," Unger said, the day they arrived. "They've got damn near as many saloons as they have people, 'n ever saloon has got near 'bout as many girls as there is customers that come into 'em."

"That sounds like quite a town," Cade agreed.

"Hey, you never found Chantal down in Galveston," Jeter said. "Maybe she's up here in Abilene."

"Could be," Cade said. Even though Jeter was Cade's closest friend, he had not told him that Arabella was Chantal.

The cook's assistant began ringing the triangle to call the cowboys to supper.

"Ha!" one of the cowboys said. "I can tell you for damn sure, that I won't be eatin' no beans 'n bacon tomorrow night. I got me a hunnert dollars comin', 'n some of it is goin' to go for a good, sit down 'n eat out of plates dinner."

"I ain't wastin' none of my money on food," another cowboy said. "I aim to get me a drink . . . no, by damn! I aim to get me a whole bottle of whiskey, then take it 'n the prettiest woman I can find, and have myself a fine ole' time."

"Hell, Duke, if you get drunk enough, it won't make no difference whether the woman is pretty or not," Slim said.

"You better watch out that some woman don't get you drunk, then take your money, 'n just TELL you what a fine time you had," Unger suggested.

The others laughed.

"Hey, Cade, you're a lot smarter 'n me," Jeter said later, when there was little chance of his being overheard. "They was 541 of the IIIX cows that made it up here. How much will that be for us?"

"I've already figured it out," Cade said. "That will be six hundred and twenty-six dollars, and twenty-five cents for each of us."

"Damn! I ain't never had that much money in my whole entire life," Jeter said. "What about you?"

"It sure is a lot of money," Cade agreed without actually answering. He thought of the money he had received from the diamonds, and also the money Arabella had taken from him. She told him she would pay him back, and he believed that she really would, if he gave her the chance.

Cade never thought he would hear himself say it, but right now he considered himself a wealthy man.

The next day Joseph McCoy came out to the bedding grounds to meet Colonel Puckett and to count the cows. The final count was four thousand one hundred and twelve.

"Here's today's prices, Colonel," McCoy said. "Buyers are paying twenty-nine fifty per head. I have to tell you, that the market has been as high as thirty one, and as low as twenty-seven. I suppose you can keep them out here and see where the market is going."

"I believe I'll take the broker's offer," Colonel Puckett said.

Abilene, as a railhead for shipping cattle, was the brainchild of Joseph McCoy. Since McCoy had brought the cattle and the railroad together, hundreds of thousands of cows had reached the Eastern markets. The town of Abilene which had only a dozen families, a few cabins, a post office, a store, and a single saloon when McCoy established it as a cattle shipping point, had ballooned into a town big enough to accommodate the business, as well as the influx of cowboys arriving in town after having spent three months on the trail. Abilene now had ten saloons, five general stores, two legitimate hotels, and two brothels, all spread out along Texas Street.

The larger, and nicer of the hotels was the Drovers Cottage and it catered to the cattle owners, trail bosses and cattle buyers. The Merchants' Hotel was less expensive and with fewer amenities than the Drovers Cottage. This is where the cowboys stayed.

Within the last several days, at least six other herds had arrived, so there were considerably more cowboys than the hotel could accommodate. That never presented a problem though, as most of the cowboys declared that they would rather save their money for liquor, gambling, and women, than spend it on sleeping.

"Hell," Slim said. "I've slept on the ground for more 'n two months, 'n I was a lot happier there, than in the saddle ridin' nighthawk. I'll just stay out here on the bedding grounds with the cattle."

Long Road to Abilene

21

ARRANGEMENTS WERE MADE to bring the cattle in to the railhead at two-hundred and fifty head per day. The trains could handle seven hundred and fifty cows per day, but the LP wasn't the only herd in Abilene. Colonel Puckett worked out a schedule whereby half the men could be in town, while the other half stayed with the herd.

Leaving the bedding grounds, Cade, Boo, and Jeter rode on into town together. The first thing Cade did was check with the post office.

"Yes sir, what can I do for you?" the mail clerk asked.

"My name is Cade McCall. I'm not sure, but I might have a letter here. If I did, it would have arrived in care of the LP herd."

The clerk smiled. "It's been here for over a month," he said.

Dear Cade,

It was with great joy that we received your letter, for we had come to think, once again, that you were dead.

There is much news to put in this letter. The first thing is the sad news that Mom has died. But, as you remember from the brief time you were here, she was no longer really with us. I believe her soul had gone on to join Papa, even before her tired, old body.

But on a happier note, you are twice an uncle. Our son, Cade Gordon is nearly two years old, and is full of vinegar. Our daughter, Margaret is as beautiful as her mother.

We have made two good crops and, with the farm paid off and secure, there is little danger of ever again getting into difficulty as we did before. And if such an occasion would come up again, it wouldn't be with Lloyd Botkins. He overextended himself, lost all his money, and has gone back to Ohio.

Melinda sends her love.

Sincerely, your brother

Adam

He put the letter in his pocket.

"From Adam?" Jeter asked. Cade had shared with Jeter than he sent Adam a letter from Ft. Worth.

"Yeah. I'm an uncle," Cade said, smiling. "I have a niece and a nephew."

Most of drovers headed for the saloons, settling in particular for the Trail's End on Texas Street, but Cade, Boo, and Jeter crossed Cedar Street where they saw a small café called Waggy's, and at Cade's suggestion they tied their horses up in front and went in.

There were three tables in the café; two were empty and a lone man sat at third. Cade and his friends took one of the other tables. An attractive, middle-aged woman came out from behind the counter.

"Yes, sir, what can I get for you men?" She asked.

"I am just betting that a place like this serves the best pie in town," Cade said.

The woman's smile grew broader. "I'm happy to say that I do get my share of compliments on the pies," she said.

"I want a piece of pie and a cup of coffee."

"What kind of pie would you like?"

"I'll let you choose."

"Yeah," Jeter said. "You can choose for me too."

"Me too," Boo added.

"That's quite a responsibility these gentlemen have put on you, Mrs. Wagner," the other customer said. "But I've no doubt but that you will choose wisely."

"I will do my best, Mr. Billingsly," Mrs. Wagner responded. "I will do my best."

"Are you three gentlemen part of an arriving herd?" Billingsly asked.

"Yes, sir, we come up here with the LP herd. The LP is a ranch down in Jackson County, Texas," Boo said.

"Southerners are you?"

"Well, yeah, Texas is south of here," Boo replied.

Billingsly chuckled. "You missed my point, young man. What I meant is, did you wear the gray during our nation's recent unpleasantness?"

"Me 'n him did," Jeter said, proudly, pointing to Cade. "We was even in the same outfit for a while. But Boo, here, he was too young."

"I'm sure you have maintained a degree of pride in having served. But I feel I would be remiss if I didn't warn you that most of the people here either fought for, or supported the Union. And many of them remember the bitter border war between Kansas and Missouri."

"Well, we didn't have anything to do with that," Cade said. "Those were irregular troops; we were with the regular army."

"I'm afraid that wouldn't make much difference to the colonel," Billingsly said.

"Who is the colonel?"

"That would be Colonel Martin Dobson. I have no way of personally validating or disproving the claim, but it is said that the colonel commanded the Fifth Ohio, a Union Regiment at Gettysburg."

"Gettysburg was a brutal battle," Cade said. "You would think that someone who saw such bloodshed would want to put it all behind him."

"One would think that, wouldn't one?" Billingsly said.

"But they would only think that if they didn't know the colonel," Mrs. Wagner said, joining the conversation as she returned from the kitchen with three small plates, and a slice of pie on each plate. "I chose dewberry," she said.

Cade smiled widely. "You chose well, ma'am. My mom used to make dewberry pie and it was my favorite."

The three had just started to eat their pie when the door opened and a man, wearing a badge, stepped into the little café.

"Hello, Deputy Tisdale," the woman said.

Cade couldn't help but notice that there was no warmth in her voice.

"Miz Wagner, the colonel sent me to see if you've got the tax money ready," the deputy said. "If you do, I can take it now."

"I have one more week before the taxes are due."

"Yes, ma'am, that's true. But here's the thing. If you ain't got the money to pay the taxes now, then that means that you more 'n likely ain't goin' to have the money to pay the taxes in another week. The colonel says to remind you of that, 'n also to remind you that his offer to buy you out still goes."

"He doesn't want to buy my place, he wants to steal it. He has offered less than half of what the café is worth," Mrs. Wagner said.

"Yeah, but remember this. If you ain't got the money come time the taxes is due, what'll happen is your café will be took away from you, 'n you won't get nothin' a' tall. You might want to think about that."

"Deputy Tisdale, do you really think I have been able to think of anything other than that?" Mrs. Wagner replied in an exasperated tone of voice.

"He told me to tell you that his offer to buy is only good up until the taxes is due. Then he'll just wait 'n take over your café' for nothin'."

"Is this colonel you are talking about so intent on getting into the restaurant business that he will harass this lady to do it?" Cade asked.

"Who are you three men?" the deputy asked.

"We're drovers with the LP. We just brought a herd up from Texas," Cade said.

"Yeah? Well what are you doing here?"

"I don't mean to be rude, Deputy, but as you can clearly see, what we are doing here is eating pie and drinking coffee."

"No, what I mean is, what are you doing on Cedar Street?"

"Obviously we are on Cedar Street, because this café is on Cedar Street."

"You've got no business bein' in here," the deputy said.

"There's no need for such harsh talk, Deputy. These three men have been perfect gentlemen from the moment they came in," Mrs. Wagner said.

"That don't matter none a' tall, 'n you know it. When they first come in, you should 'a told 'em what the law was."

"What law?" Cade asked, surprised by the comment.

"The law that says that the only place that drovers can be is either at the stockyard, in the Merchants' Hotel, or in one of the stores or saloons on Texas Street. This here is Cedar Street, 'n you ain't allowed here."

"That's not a law, Deputy Tisdale, and you know it," Mrs. Wagner said.

"Maybe it ain't a law, but it's a rule the colonel has put out."

"Who is this colonel that he can put out a rule that doesn't have the authority of the law?" Cade asked.

"Colonel Dobson runs this here town," Tisdale said.

"You are an officer of the law. Are you saying that the colonel controls you?"

"Ah, but you have put your finger on the rub, gentleman. Disabuse yourself of any idea that Ron Tisdale is an officer of the law," Billingsly said. "Despite the badge he is wearing, he has no administrative authority. He is merely one of Colonel Dobson's lackeys."

Tilsdale pointed at Billingsly. "You'd better watch your mouth, Billingsly. You saw what happened when you spoke out against the colonel the last time."

"I didn't 'speak out' my good man, I expressed my views as an editorial in my newspaper, THE DEFIANT. Evidently, the colonel is unaware of the First Amendment to the United States Constitution, the one that guarantees freedom of the press."

"You should 'a paid your taxes on time," Tisdale said. "And the same thing goes for you, Miz Wagner. You don't pay your taxes, and you'll be losing this café, same as Billingsly lost his newspaper."

"Did I understand you right, when you said that Tisdale has no administrative authority?" Cade asked.

"That's right. Tisdale here, is a deputy for Colonel Martin Dobson, who is himself without administrative legal sanction."

"What kind of town is this where a private citizen can have his own deputies?" Cade asked.

"You would need to know what kind of man the colonel is, in order to understand that," Billingsly explained. "He is the kind of man that would take advantage of any opportunity that might present itself. You see, Colonel Dobson realized that the influx of cattle was going to do two things. One, it was going to bring a boisterous group of young men into a town that had no law. It also meant that this same event would mean the infusion of a great deal of money into our economy.

"The colonel organized a private detective agency and had it licensed by the state. That gave him limited police powers, but it wasn't necessary for him to go beyond those limited powers in order to accomplish what he wanted.

"By a rather bizarre interpretation of the law of eminent domain, it also gave him the authority to levy a tax against all the businesses; supposedly to pay for the 'protection' his detective agency provides the town. It was that, my railing against these levied taxes' that led to the colonel shutting down my newspaper."

"Them stories you wrote in the paper had nothing to do with it," Tisdale said. "You was shut down 'cause you didn't pay your taxes. The colonel is running the paper now."

"Yes, and a once-proud beacon of truth has become an organ of lies and self-aggrandizement," Billingsly said, bitterly.

Tisdale turned his attention away from Billingsly, and glared once more at Cade and the others. The three men had been following, with interest, the conversation, but that had not interfered with their enjoying the pie.

"What's your name, cowboy?" Tisdale asked.

"McCall. Cade McCall."

"McCall, are you and your friends going to leave here, 'n get back on Texas Street where you belong, or am I going to have to get some more deputies 'n run you out of here?"

"Well, I do want to get a drink, so I guess we'll leave."

"Good. You'll be savin' yourself a lot of trouble."

"But we're not ready to go just yet," Cade said.

"Now why do you want to go ag'in the town like that?"

"I thought it was the colonel we were going against."

"Goin' ag'in the colonel IS goin' ag'in the town," Tisdale said. "That's 'cause the colonel IS the town."

"I'll just bet that Mrs. Wagner and Mr. Billingsly don't agree with you that the colonel is the town," Cade challenged.

"I certainly do not agree," Billingsly said.

"And I expect there are many others in town who don't agree as well," Cade said.

"If you go to stirrin' up this town, you're just goin' to cause trouble for yourself," Tidale said. "Maybe I should take care of this now. There's two more deputies, not more'n a hunnert yards from here. I can have them here in less than a minute."

Cade lifted his cup and took a drink of his coffee, his demeanor one of total dispassion.

"Two more won't be enough, Tisdale," Cade said easily.

Tisdale stood for several more seconds. With the power of the colonel and all the deputies behind him, he was used to evoking fear in others. The serenity of this man had instilled fear in him.

"All right," he finally said. "But once you finish your pie and coffee, you three get on over to Texas Street where you belong, so as not to cause any trouble for the decent folks."

The deputy left the café and Billingsly let out a loud guffaw. "I haven't enjoyed anything that much since Bessie June pushed Silas Crabtree out her window, and he fell into the watering trough. You were magnificent!"

"You were indeed," Mrs. Wagner said. She smiled broadly. "Your coffee and pie are on the house."

"No, now, we couldn't do that," Jeter said. "We heard you 'n the deputy talkin'. How you goin' to pay your taxes, if you go around givin' away your pie 'n coffee?"

Mrs. Wagner laughed. "Your pie is ten cents apiece, the coffee is a nickel. I owe fifty dollars in taxes. Forty-five cents isn't going to break me, nor is it going to pay my taxes."

"Millie, I told you not to worry about those taxes," Billingsly said. "I'm going to help you pay them."

"I appreciate the offer, George, I really do," Millie said. "But you didn't even have enough money to save your own newspaper. There is no way I would prevail upon you to help me save my café."

"Ah, but coward that I am, I sold out before my newspaper was confiscated. Because of that, I'm not totally bereft of funds. I said I would help you, and I will. I just want Dobson to have the false anticipation that he is going to have his way."

Long Road to Abilene

22

IT WAS MID-MORNING when Cade, Jeter and Boo stepped into the Trail's End Saloon, but despite the early hour, the saloon was full and noisy. The bar was packed with cowboys. not only from the LP but from the other herds that had been brought to Abilene in the last several days.Behind the bar was a painting of a reclining naked woman. Over time, several would-be marksmen had tried to augment the painting by putting bullet holes in strategic places. Most had missed.

Duke and Lefty were at the bar, Unger and Slim were at the gaming table, Rufus and Ian were sitting at one of the tables.

"Cade, would ye 'n the lads be for joining us?" Ian called.

"We'll be right there as soon as we get a drink," Cade replied.

"Sure now, 'n there's NAE need to mingle with the uncivilized crowd at the bar. The young lass will bring your drinks."

"All right," Cade said. Because there were three of them, Boo had to take a chair from an adjoining table.

"Damn, you're all cleaned up," Jeter said.

"Aye, for 'tis no heathen I am. The first thing I did when reaching this wee village was to get a bath 'n a shave."

"You said something about us being able to get a drink?" Cade said.

"Aye, I did, didn't I, lad? Bessie June!" Ian called.

An attractive young woman approached the table, wearing a revealing costume and a practiced smile.

"What will it be, gents?" Bessie June asked.

"As long as it isn't what you served Silas Crabtree just before you pushed him through the window," Cade replied, returning Bessie June's smile.

"My goodness is there anybody in Kansas who hasn't heard of that?"

"You may as well get used to it, you're a famous woman," Cade said.

"I suppose I am. So, what do you handsome but unwashed," she paused and, with a smile, pinched her nose, "gentlemen want this famous woman to bring you?"

"A beer will be fine."

"NAE!" Ian said, holding up his hand. "A heathen place this is, to be sure, but 'tis a decent scotch they have. 'N would you be for tellin' me why anyone would drink anything else?"

Cade laughed. "Scotch it will be, then."

Bessie June retuned quickly with the scotch, and when Cade tipped her, she made a little curtsey toward him. "Now I feel bad that I said something about you being unwashed."

"No need to feel bad about it," Cade said. "We are unwashed, but I intend to correct that condition after a drink or two."

Their conversation was interrupted by a loud shout from the gaming table. "You cheating son of a bitch!"

The shout was followed by gunfire from at least three guns. The drover who had called out went down under the gunfire.

The victim was obviously a drover, but he wasn't someone from the LP herd. The three who had shot him, all of them wearing a star on their shirts, approached and stood there for a long moment, the smoking pistols still in their hands.

"All right," one of them shouted. "Get back to your business. We'll take care of this."

"For a town that's so wee, 'tis strange to see that Abilene has so many in its constabulary," Ian said.

"Constabulary?" Boo asked.

"Gentlemen of the law," Ian explained, nodding toward one of the three men wearing badges. "There are three in here, 'n there were three in the first pub we visited. If there are as many in every pub in town, 'twould mean at least thirty."

"They are not gentlemen, and they are not the law," Cade said.

"They aren't the law?" Rufus asked.

"Not real law, they ain't," Jeter said. "They're private detectives."

"I've heard of private detectives, but not like this," Rufus said. "What are they? Railroad detectives? Pinkerton agents?"

"Nothing that legitimate," Cade said. "They work for a man named Dobson."

"Colonel Dobson," Jeter said. "Don't forget, he was a blue belly colonel."

Colonel Dobson's office was upstairs over the Cattleman's Bank. His desk, of carved oak, sat on the far side of the room. The large office intimidated his visitors who would have to cross the space between the desk and the door.

Dobson had done well for himself, arriving in Abilene shortly after Joseph McCoy began to institute his plan of making Abilene a railhead for shipping cattle. Dobson was quick to recognize the brilliance of McCoy's plan, and while

McCoy would be making money in handling cattle, Dobson would make money by handling people.

"The town is going to grow fast," Dobson told McCoy. "It's also going to attract a rough crowd of men, who will want to celebrate the end of a long cattle drive. If we have no law to control such men, they could destroy everything you're trying to build."

"I'm afraid you're right," McCoy had said. "I guess I didn't think that far. We won't be able to depend on the county sheriff and we have no law in the town."

"I'll supply the law," Dobson told McCoy, explaining his idea of using a private detective agency.

When Dobson got a license to operate his private detective agency as a city police force, he also got the authority to assess a tax on all the businesses of the town. Now, he was contemplating a new source of income, and he was talking it over with Enos Crites. Crites was the chief of the private police.

He was also a seasoned gunfighter who had faced down, and killed, many men.

"I want you to go down to the holding pens and see McCoy," Crites said. "Tell him he is to collect a fee of fifty cents per head from every cow that ships out from Abilene."

"All right," Crites said.

There was a knock on the office door.

"Colonel, may I come in?" Tisdale called.

"Yes, Crites was just leaving. Did you collect the taxes From Millie Wagner?"

"She said she didn't have the money."

Dobson smiled. "I didn't expect she would have. Looks like I'll be going into the restaurant business."

"There's something else," Tisdale said.

"What is it?"

Tisdale told about encountering the three drovers in Waggy's Café. "They were former Confederate soldiers. Sometimes they act like they was the ones that won the war. I told 'em they couldn't be in Waggy's, that they had to keep themselves on Texas Street, but they wasn't too happy about it. I've got a feelin' them three might wind up givin' us some trouble."

"I pay you to take care of trouble. Did they go to Texas Street?"

"Yeah, they went, all right."

Tisdale didn't mention that they had called his bluff, moving on their own time.

"Then what makes you think those three men, in particular, are going to give us any trouble?"

"Actually, it may just be one of 'em," Tisdale said. "I expect he's the one the other two listen to. Leastwise, he's the one that did all the talkin'."

"Does the talker have a name?"

"Oh, yeah, he has a name all right. Cade McCall, he says he is."

"Cade McCall?" Colonel Dobson said, showing some interest in the name.

"Yeah, why, do you know him?"

"No, how would I know him?" Dobson replied, quickly. "But if you think he is going to be a troublemaker, maybe you should find a reason to see to it that he doesn't have the opportunity."

"What do you mean, charge fifty cents per head? What in the hell is Dobson thinking about?" McCoy asked. "After everything else these men have been through, almost three months on the trail; storms, stampedes, Indians, rustlers, drought, and you expect them to pay the city fifty cents a head taxes when they get here?"

"They'll pay it," Crites said.

"They may not pay it."

"What are they going to do, take the cows back?" Crites asked with a mocking laugh.

"Well if Dobson wants to charge fifty cents a head, he is going to have to take it up with the owners and trail bosses himself. I have absolutely no intention of doing it."

"The colonel isn't going to like that."

"The colonel is doing all right for himself. I'm sure he will adjust."

"Mr. McCoy?" someone called. "The broker is here for the T bar S herd."

"I'll be right there," McCoy replied. "If you will excuse me, Mr. Crites?"

Crites watched McCoy walk away, then he remounted for the ride back into town to report to the colonel on what McCoy said. He found Dobson having his lunch in a private dining room at the Drovers Cottage.

"McCoy says he won't do it," Crites said.

Dobson buttered a roll.

"You weren't persuasive enough," Dobson said.

"I know people. And I know that no matter how persuasive I get, McCoy won't change his mind."

"I see."

"Look, I've already told you how I feel about McCoy. Why don't you just let me kill the son of a bitch, and that way we can take over the whole operation?"

"That's what you think, is it?"

"Yeah, that's what I think."

"Clearly, you haven't thought it through, Mr. Crites. Remember, it was McCoy who arranged for the cattle to come here in the first place. He is also the one who talked the railroad into coming here, and he is the one who made the deal with the meat packers. Without McCoy there would be no more cattle business, and without the cattle business, this whole town would wither and die on the vine. No, sir, I will not kill the goose that lays the golden egg."

Leaving Dobson at his meal, Crites passed through the dining room of the hotel. Here, cattle owners, brokers, and railroad officials were enjoying the finest cuisine Abilene had to offer. And though Dobson paid Crites enough money to eat here if he wanted, this wasn't for him. They served food at the Trail's End Saloon, and he had a private table there. That's where he would have lunch.

For the next two days Cade, Jeter, and Boo had to stay out at the bedding grounds. The work was very easy, there was no need to drive the herd and the cows had settled in, comfortable with the grass and the water. The cowboys merely rode, lazily, around the herd by day, and were even less active by night.

When Cade, Jeter, Boo, and Rufus went back to town, the first place they went was a barber shop where all four had a bath and a shave. From there, they went to Baker Clothiers to buy new duds.

"What do you think?" Boo asked. He held one leg out to show off his calfskin boots coming up to just below the knees, cut off square on the top and with "mule-ear" tugs hanging down each side. They were high heeled, with a red star at the top.

"When the women see me in these boots, they won't be able to keep their hands offen me."

"Ha!" Jeter said. "How much did them boots cost you? Three fifty? You can go into any saloon in town and pick up a woman for two dollars."

"Yeah, but then the two dollars will be gone," Boo said. "I'll still have these boots."

Rufus laughed. "I think the boy has you on that one, Jeter."

Cade glanced toward the wall clock. "Hey, it's nearly noon. Why don't we go get dinner?"

"Waggy's?" Jeter asked.

Cade smiled. "Why not?"

"We're not supposed to be there, that's why not," Boo said.

"Well, that was when we were drovers with nothing but trail dust and dirty clothes. But we're all cleaned up and wearing new clothes now," Cade said. "You might say we are quality folks in these parts, and in these times."

Millie Wagner looked up when the four men walked in. After a few seconds she flashed them a welcoming smile.

"My!" she said. "I almost didn't recognize you gentlemen."

"You just didn't recognize us 'cause last time we was wearin' old clothes, 'n now we're wearin' new duds," Boo said.

"It probably also makes a difference that we don't smell like cows now," Cade added.

"There are four of you this time," Millie said, looking toward Rufus.

"This is our cook," Jeter said. "If you got 'ny more o' that dewberry pie, I want him to try it out after dinner. Maybe he can fix it for us out on the trail sometime."

Millie laughed, then led the men over to an empty table. It wasn't hard to find a place to sit, all three of the tables were empty because there was no one in the café.

"You are open, aren't you, Mrs. Wagner?" Cade asked. "Maybe we should have checked with you."

"I'm open."

"Oh, I just thought that since it's dinner time, there'd be a crowd here."

"Since Dobson passed the law that no drovers can leave Texas Street, you ARE the dinner crowd," she said.

23

VAN BEECHER WALKED out of Baker Clothier with a buoyant bounce to his step. He was wearing new trousers, shirt, and boots, but he was most proud of his new hat, a black, high – crown Stetson. He took it off to look at it again, smiling in the pride of ownership.

"Hey, you! Cowboy! Get back on Texas Street where you belong!" someone shouted.

"There ain't nothin' on Texas Street that I want to see," Van answered. "Why should I go there?"

The man who had issued the order was wearing a star on his vest. "Because I told you to go there."

"And I told you there ain't nothin' on Texas Street I want to see."

"I'm an officer of the law," the deputy said. "Now how is it goin' to look to the others if I give an order, 'n it ain't obeyed?"

"Mister, the only ones who can give me orders are Colonel Puckett 'n Rufus Slade."

"You're wearin' a gun," the deputy said. "Either get over on Texas Street like I told you, or pull that gun."

"What? You would shoot me because I'm not on the right street?"

"Nah, I'm goin' to shoot you 'cause you didn't obey my order. Now, get over on Texas Street like I tole you."

"No."

"Then pull your gun."

"I ain't a' goin' to do that neither. If you shoot me it's goin' to be just flat out murder, 'n I don't think you want any of these good folk who are lookin' on to see that."

The deputy drew his pistol and fired, his bullet taking off Van's right earlobe.

Van let out a cry of pain, and put his hand to his shredded ear. "What the hell did you do that for?"

"Draw," the deputy said.

"I ain't a'goin' to draw on you."

The deputy drew, and fired again. This time the bullet hit Van in the fleshy part of his left leg, about six inches above the knee.

Now Van was holding his right hand over his ear, and his left hand over the bullet hole in his leg. Blood poured through the fingers of both hands.

"Are you crazy?" Van shouted. "Why are you shootin' at me like that?"

"I'm tryin' to get you to man up so you'll fight back. I'll let you draw first," the deputy said, his pistol now back in his holster. He smiled. "I tell you what, I won't even draw 'til you got your gun out."

"No."

"Suit yourself, you don't have to draw if you don't want to. You can just stand there 'n let me cut you to pieces,"

"Ahhhh!" Van screamed making a desperate grab for his pistol.

The deputy watched, amused by the awkwardness of the draw. He waited until the gun was level before he started his own draw. He pulled his pistol and fired in one quick motion and Van Beecher, with a look of surprise, fell face down onto the boardwalk.

"You shouldn't ought to have done that, Deputy Tisdale," one of the witnesses said.

"You seen it," Tisdale replied. "He drew on me first."

Slim, Duke, and Lefty had left the Trail's End on an exploratory tour of the other saloons. Jess Unger and Ian Campbell of the LP were still in the Trail's End saloon. Three of the cattle outfits, having completed all their business, were now on their way back to Texas, and that left only the LP and the Rocking K still in town.

At the moment, Campbell and Unger represented one half of all the paying customers in Trail's End. The other half being from the Rocking K. There were two more men in the saloon, but they weren't paying customers. They were deputies, and as such were entitled to free drinks.

Bessie June sat at a table in the back of the saloon, playing a game of solitaire. Earlier she had engaged in a little pleasant conversation with the four drovers, but there clearly weren't enough customers in the saloon to require her services.

"How long do you reckon it'll be 'a fore you fellers start back?" one of the Rocking K men asked.

"I don't reckon we'll be here much longer," Unger said. "What with most of the other herds gone, we can put about seven hunnert 'n fifty cows on the cars a day, so I expect we'll be pullin' out pretty soon."

"We'll more 'n likely be right behind you," the Rocking K cowboy said. "We got started later 'n you all did, but we're puttin' on as many cows each day as ya'll are."

Another customer came in then. The new customer was not a cowboy, but a resident of the community. When he stepped up to the bar he was standing about six feet down from Campbell and Unger.

"I need a drink, Hodge," he said to the bartender. "I ain't never seen nothin' like it."

The bartender poured the customer a glass of whiskey and pushed it across the bar.

"What did you see, Tim?" Hodge asked.

Tim tossed the drink down before he replied.

"Tisdale just shot 'n killed a cowboy for no reason at all. 'N here's the thing. It turns out that the cowboy wasn't nothin' but a kid. Hell, he couldn't a been more 'n fifteen or sixteen."

"Son of a bitch," Unger said, having overheard the conversation. "Ian, do you reckon that might a' been . . .?"

Unger didn't finish the question because Campbell interrupted with a question of his own, directed not at Unger, nor even at the man who had brought the news. He questioned the two drovers from the Rocking K.

"Would yer outfit be for havin' a wee lad who is still a boy, such as that described by the mon here?"

The two glanced at each other before one of them answered.

"If the drover the deputy shot is as young as the man says, there's no way he can belong to us. We don't have a man who is under twenty – two, maybe twenty – three years old."

"It had to be Van!" Unger said.

"Aye, 'could be no other," Campbell agreed.

Van's body was put in an open coffin and stood up in front of the Shockey and Landes Hardware store. A sign over the body read:

DO YOU KNOW THIS ~~MAN?~~ Boy

It was an act of frustrated defiance that had driven someone to strike through the word man, and replace it with boy.

"His name is Van Beecher," Cade told the undertaker. "Now, get him down from there. He was our friend, and I'll not have him on display like some carnival freak."

"I'm sorry, mister, I meant no disrespect," the undertaker replied. "I was just hoping we could get him identified, is all."

Cade didn't have to ask the undertaker how it happened. He had already heard the story as to how Deputy Tisdale baited him, then shot him.

Campbell and Unger were there as well.

"Cade, if you can take care of everything here, Jess and I will take the sad news to Colonel Puckett 'n the others so that we can be for having services for the lad," Campbell said.

"Yes, go tell the colonel," Cade said.

Cade made arrangements with the undertaker for Van to be buried the next day.

"We'll be needing a preacher," Cade said.

"I'm sure you could get Reverend Luscomb to do the funeral."

"Thank you. Make the arrangements, please."

The next day, Van's body was transported to the graveyard in a shining ebony, glass sided, hearse. The hearse was pulled by four white horses each horse draped with a purple pall, their manes adorned by a black feather plume. A considerable number of the citizens of the town lined both sides of the street as the hearse made its way to the cemetery.

For the actual interment, every LP drover was there. Nearly all the Rocking K drovers were there as well. They considered Van one of their own, simply because, like them, he had helped bring a herd up from Texas.

George Billingsly was present for the burial and so was Millie Wagner. Arnold Baker, who owned the clothier where Van had bought the clothes that he was being buried in, was there as well. The shirt, which had a bullet hole and was stained with blood, had been replaced with one that was identical, free of charge by Baker.

Six of the LP riders, using ropes, carefully lowered the coffin into the grave. When that was done, the preacher, wearing a black suit, white shirt, and black string tie, said a few words, asking that nobody's blood be boiling over with the craving of revenge, reading from the Bible, Romans 12:19: "DEARLY BELOVED, AVENGE NOT YOURSELVES, BUT RATHER GIVE PLACE UNTO WRATH: FOR IT IS WRITTEN, VENGEANCE IS MINE; I WILL REPAY, SAITH THE LORD."

After the funeral, most of the LP drovers returned to the bedding grounds outside of town. Cade, Jeter, Rufus and Boo went to Waggy's where Millie Wagner served pie and coffee, for a repast. George Billingsly was there as well.

"What kind of man is Tisdale that he could shoot down a boy like that?" Cade asked

"He is typical of the kind of man who now controls every aspect of our lives," Billingsly replied. "All the deputies have a background with guns, every one of them. That's why Dobson hired them in the first place. None have quite the reputation of our illustrious chief of police, but they are all quite skilled in the art of killing."

"Who is your chief of police?" Jeter asked.

"He's the worst of them all," Billingsly said. "His name is Enos Crites."

"Who?" Rufus asked, quickly.

"Enos Crites," Billingsly repeated.

"I wondered where he would wind up."

"Rufus, do you know Crites?" Cade asked.

"I used to know him. We were friends, once. Then he began selling his gun to the wrong people and I lost touch with him."

"What I don't understand is what Van could have possibly been doing that set this off," Boo said. "He was just a real nice kid, he never gave nobody any trouble."

"He was killed because he wasn't on Texas Street," Billingsly said. "Arnold Baker watched it all from the front door of his store. Tisdale ordered him back onto Texas Street, but the boy refused. Then, according to Baker, Tisdale just began shooting, taking nicks out of him until finally the boy had no choice but to draw his own gun. And that's when Tisdale killed him."

"That is awful. Just awful," Millie said.

"Yes it is. And this has gone far enough," Billingsly said. "I think it is high time that the people do something about it, and believe me, if I still had my newspaper, I would print a first page editorial condemning Dobson and all his mignons in the harshest possible terms."

"Is your newspaper still here?" Cade asked. "What I mean is, is there still a press, ink, and paper?"

"The noble press of Abilene has died, but the ghost of the paper remains. To answer your question, yes the paper is still here, but now it belongs to Dobson, and as I said, it is used by him as a self-serving tool."

"We're going to use it," Cade said. "Show me where it is, Mr. Billingsly. We are going to take the paper back so that you can print whatever you wish."

When Cade and Billingsly stepped into the newspaper office a few minutes later, their arrival was announced by a bell, its ring activated by opening the front door. They were met by a rather small man, bald headed, and with a closely trimmed moustache that didn't extend beyond the ends of his mouth.

"Mr. Billingsly! What are you doing here, sir? I thought you said you would never set foot in here again."

"Hello, Mr. Lovelace. As you can see, I have changed my mind."

Lovelace, who had been working in the back, was wearing an ink-stained apron.

"What caused you to change your mind?"

"Perhaps you heard of the young man that Deputy Tisdale shot down in the street, today."

"I heard something about it, yes. I haven't heard any of the details."

"Well, I *have* heard the details, and I think everyone in town should hear the details."

Billingsly turned toward Cade and the others who had come into the newspaper office with him.

"Mr. McCall, this is Paul Lovelace. He was my compositor, and when I lost my newspaper, he stayed on to work for the enemy."

"Mr. Billingsly, I had no choice!" Lovelace complained. "I have a family to feed and I have no other employable skill."

"I'm not angry with you, Paul. In fact, you'll have a chance to make it up to me. I'm about to put out a special edition of THE DEFIANT, and you can print it for me."

"But how are you going to do that? This isn't your newspaper anymore," Lovelace said.

"Let's just say that I have re-acquired the newspaper. If you want to leave now so you can tell Dobson you had nothing to do with it, I'm quite capable of putting the paper out myself."

Since Billingsly and the others had arrived, the expressions on Lovelace's face had mirrored confusion and fear. Now he showed defiance and determination.

"No, sir, you won't have to put the paper out by yourself. I would be proud to compose it for you."

"Very well, Mr. Lovelace, get the type sticks ready and let's get this paper on the street," Billingsly said, enthusiastically.

"He was just a boy," Dobson said. "What in the hell were you thinking about when you shot him down like that?"

"Colonel, we've got a whole town here to deal with," Tisdale replied. "And nearly 'bout ever' damn one of 'em was in the war. Maybe they don't carry guns no more, 'n maybe most of 'em is tryin' to forget the war, but we can't show them no weakness at all, else they might figure out that they could all get together 'n fight us. 'N we can't take on the whole town.

"You asked why I shot 'im? I shot 'im 'cause he didn't obey my order when I told him to get back onto Texas Street. And we can't none of us afford to have people just pay no never mind to our orders. Crites, you said yourself that we needed to let people know who was in charge here."

"I said that," Crites said. "I'm not sure that shooting a boy would do that."

"How the hell was I supposed to know how old he was? He was a drover, he was wearin' a gun, 'n he wasn't on Texas Street where he belonged."

"Colonel, if you was to take back the order 'bout keepin' all the cowboys on Texas Street, that problem wouldn't come up no more," Parker suggested.

The discussion, involving Tisdale, Parker, Crites, and Dobson, was taking place in Dobson's office.

"No, we have to keep the cowboys on Texas Street," Dobson said. "There are ten saloons there, and we get a nice piece of that pie."

"Some of the merchants that's not on Texas Street is complainin' that they're losin' business," Parker said.

"They're making money from the brokers, the cattle owners, and the trail bosses," Dobson said. "The drovers don't have that much money, and we need them to spend the money they do have in the saloons and whorehouses."

"Tisdale, tell me them names that you said again," Crites asked.

"What names?"

"You said somethin' about the boy tellin' you that he only took orders from two people. Who were the two people?"

"One was Colonel Puckett. I don't recall the other name."

"You said the other name a while ago."

"Yeah, well, it was still fresh in my mind then. Right now I can't recollect."

"Was it Cade McCall?" Dobson asked.

"No, I would have remembered it if it had been McCall. He's the one I run into in Waggy's, remember? It was somebody else."

"I believe you said Rufus Slade," Crites said, cryptically.

"Yes, that's it. He said he only took orders from Colonel Puckett and Rufus Slade. How the hell is it you was able to remember that name, when I couldn't?"

"I've heard the name before," Crites said.

"Does that name mean anything to you?" Dobson asked.

"If it's the same person I'm thinking about, yeah, it means something. The only thing, he's about the last person I would picture as a drover."

"Well, who is he?"

Crites made a dismissive wave of his hand.

"Never mind, it can't be the same person."

"Colonel, the town is a little jumpy," Parker said. "Did you see how many turned out for this boy's wake? I mean they was lined up on both sides of the street, 'n it wasn't 'cause they was just curious neither. If you was to ask me, I'd say we're goin' to have to kind of keep a pretty close watch on these folks."

"I agree. The drovers come and go, but the townspeople are here all the time. It might be necessary for us to remind them of just who is in charge here."

24

THAT AFTERNOON THE CITIZENS of Abilene saw something they hadn't seen in the last six months. They saw an issue of THE DEFIANT. Billingsly printed 500 copies of the paper then put them out all over town, free of charge. Word spread quickly that the newspaper was back in circulation, and within no time at all, every copy had been picked up.

Shop keepers shared the information with their customers, barbers talked about it with their clients, ladies discussed it in their garden clubs.

"Did you see that THE DEFIANT is back?"

"How is that possible? I thought Mr. Billingsly lost the newspaper."

"Maybe he started a new one."

Millie Wagner was the very first to see the paper because Billingsly brought her a copy even before the others were distributed.

"Oh, George, I don't know if this was such a good idea," she said. "I'm afraid for you."

"To quote the great bard, Millie, 'A coward dies a thousand times before his death, but the valiant taste of death but once.'"

"That's what Amos said before he left to go to war. He died at Antietam, a place I had never heard of."

"Your husband was a brave man who did his duty. I make no claim to be as brave, but I have a duty to do as well," George said.

It was one of Dobson's deputies who brought him a copy of the newspaper, though because it was only one page, and contained only one story, it could more properly be referred to as a broadside, rather than a newspaper.

"Colonel, maybe you need to see this," the deputy said, handing the single sheet to Dobson.

AN ASSERTION OF THE RIGHTS OF THE CITIZENS OF ABILENE

"When in the Course of human events, it becomes necessary for one people to dissolve the political bands which have connected them with another, and to assume among the powers of the earth, the separate and equal station to which the Laws of Nature and of Nature's God entitle them, a decent respect to the opinions of mankind requires that they should declare the causes which impel them to the separation."

Thus begins the Declaration of Independence by which this nation was born. The trials, tribulations, and travails which were visited upon the people of the colonies are repeated here, in Abilene. Our oppression comes not from a government whose deliberative body has passed laws, but from a single, evil despot who has employed thirty gunmen to enforce his unholy will upon an innocent body of people.

As the owner and publisher of this newspaper, I must confess that I surrendered to the unjust demand that I give up my newspaper, and in so doing relinquished my self-respect. It is my intention by this publication to regain my dignity, and to instill in those who read these words, a determination to do the same.

The catalyst of this resolve was the senseless and brutal murder of a fourteen year old boy, shot down on the street by Ron Tisdale, a "deputy" in Colonel Dobson's malevolent private detective agency. The young man's name was Van Beecher, and his crime was to have purchased clothes from a store on Mulberry Street, rather than whisky on Texas Street.

It is high time that this charlatan "police force" be eliminated, and replaced by legally constituted, city government mandated officers of the law.

With this publication, I call upon all who honor freedom, to unite in resolve to overthrow the tyranny that has, for too long, oppressed our citizenry.

And to this story I append my name: George W. Billingsly.

"How did he do this?" Dobson asked. "Where did Billingsly get this printed?"

"From what I've heard, he done it at the newspaper office."

"But I own that newspaper!" Dobson said, angrily.

"Yes, sir, you do. But that's where this here paper was done."

"Find Tisdale and tell him to take care this."

Billingsly was showing Cade around the newspaper office.

"I should have never given it up," he said. "I should have stayed here and fought Dobson. I'm ashamed that I sold the paper to him."

"How much did he pay you for it?" Cade asked.

"One hundred and fifty dollars," he said. "The building and equipment alone are worth at least five hundred dollars. I would say that the good name of the paper was worth an equal amount, but he didn't continue with THE DEFIANT. He began publishing something he called, THE ORDER.

"I will loan you one hundred and fifty dollars to buy the newspaper back," Cade offered.

"You've got that much money?" Billingsly asked, then he held up his hand and shook his head. "Forgive me, Mr. McCall. I had no right to blurt that out. That is most generous of you, and if I thought Dobson would accept it, I would take you up on your offer."

Cade smiled. "I have a feeling that after what you printed and circulated today, that Dobson won't be around much longer. I think the people of Abilene will answer your call to overthrow the tyrant."

"From your lips to God's ear," Billingsly replied.

The two men had been in the press room when they heard a shot from the front of the office. Hurrying to the sound, they saw Deputy Tisdale standing there holding a smoking pistol in his hand. Paul Lovelace was on the floor with a hole in his chest. The ubiquitous apron now had more blood than ink.

"Paul! Paul!" Billingsly shouted kneeling beside the man who had worked with him for so long.

"Mr. Billingsly, I'm glad you . . ."

Whatever Lovelace planned to say died with him, as he took his last, rattling breath.

"Tisdale! What did you do?" Billingsly shouted in anguish and anger. "This was murder!"

"No it warn't. I shot 'im for not obeyin' an order. Same as when I shot that drover."

"What order did Mr. Lovelace disobey?"

"I ordered him not to print no more newspapers, 'n he said he was workin' for you again, 'n he would put together as many newspapers as you wanted to print. The colonel told me to make sure the paper don't get printed no more, 'n I figure now that there ain't nobody to put the thing together, there won't be no more paper." Arrogantly, confidently, Tisdale put the gun back in its holster.

"You figured wrong. I intend to buy back this newspaper and when I get it back, I'll be Dobson's worst nightmare."

Tisdale's mouth spread into an evil smile. "No you won't," he said. "On account if you don't leave here now, you'll join your friend on the floor."

"I'm not armed," Billingsly said.

The evil smile grew broader. "Yeah? Well, that didn't stop me from shootin' Lovelace, did it?"

"I don't know if you noticed, Tisdale, but I AM armed," Cade said, speaking for the first time. He was standing by the door that led back into the press room.

"Yeah, you are, ain't you?" Tisdale said. "You wantin' to take me on, do you, cowboy?"

"I will if I have to. The boy you killed was a friend of mine. Mr. Lovelace was a friend of Mr. Billingsly, and Mr. Billingsly is a friend of mine. I don't intend to just stand here and . . ."

Without warning, Tisdale drew his gun and fired at Cade. Cade's first reaction at seeing Tisdale go for his gun was not to draw, but to twist his body out of the way, denying Tisdale a target.

The bullet from Tisdale's gun slammed into the doorframe just behind where Cade had been standing but an instant earlier. By now Cade had his own pistol drawn, and even as he was drawing his gun, he could recall the words of Rufus:

"Here's your first lesson. It isn't who shoots first; it is who hits what he is shooting at first."

Cade squeezed the trigger and felt the gun buck in his hand. A puff of dust erupted from Tisdale's dirty shirt where the bullet hit. The deputy's eyes grew wide in shock and he cupped his hand over the bullet wound, then pulled it away to see it filling with blood.

"I'll be damn."

Those were his last words as he fell back through the door and on to the boardwalk in front of the newspaper office.

Word of Tisdale being killed spread quickly through the town and within moments more than a score of people were gathered around Tisdale's body including two of the deputies.

"Who shot this man?" one of the deputies asked.

"I did," Billingsly said.

"No, I did," Cade said.

"I did!" one of the townspeople said.

"No, I did!" another said, and soon more than a dozen men "confessed" to being the one who shot Tisdale.

Frustrated, the deputies left, their retreat followed by the derisive laughter of those who had gathered around the newspaper office.

Not until the undertaker had claimed the bodies of both Paul Lovelace and Ron Tisdale did the crowd in front of the newspaper office disperse.

Cade left as well, and joined Jeter, Boo, and Rufus at Trail's End. The four of them were now the only LP riders left in town, Campbell, Unger, and the others having returned to the bedding ground. A couple citizens of the town who had been part of the gathering outside the newspaper office, earlier were also customers at the saloon. The two deputies who had been at the scene of the shooting were there as well, and they were sitting together at a table in the back corner, glaring at Cade and the others.

"Hey, you," one of the deputies called to Cade. "You're one of them who said you kilt Tisdale, ain't you?"

Cade turned toward the two deputies.

"It was you that actual done it, wasn't it? I mean all those other'n said it was them, but I know it was you."

"You're presence isn't welcome here," Cade said. "I think you two men need to find some other place to be."

"Colonel Dobson told us to stay here," one of them replied.

"I'm telling you to leave. And you might have noticed that I'm here and Dobson isn't."

The two men looked at each other for a moment, then got up and left the saloon.

Bessie June had been standing with one of the other girls, at the far end of the bar. "Well now," she said with a big smile. "Hodge, you are about to see something that's never happened before. Instead of a customer buying a bar girl a drink, this bar girl wants to buy a customer a drink. Give that handsome gentleman with the rusty hair a drink on me."

"I'm much obliged to you, ma'am," Cade replied.

"Are you the one who talked Billingsly into printing that paper?" the bartender asked as he poured a new drink for Cade.

"No, Mr. Billingsly came up with that idea all by himself."

"I'll bet he don't have no idea of what all he has stirred up," the bartender said. "I've heard talk. I think folks are about ready to throw Dobson and his men out of town."

Crites had just stepped out of the Hog Waller Saloon when he saw the two deputies leave the Trail's End. Curious as to why they would leave before he told them to, he crossed the street and looked over the top of the batwing doors.

"I'll be damn," he said under his breath. "It is Slade."

"He run us out of the saloon," one of the two deputies said.

"Who ran you out?" Dobson asked.

"The feller that kilt Tisdale. Only it warn't just him, they was four of 'em. We didn't have no choice, Colonel."

"You were smart to leave when you did," Crites said. "Rufus Slade was with them."

"That's the second time you've mentioned that name, Rufus Slade," Dobson said. "Do you know him?"

"Yeah, I know him," Crites said. "Me 'n him used to work together some."

"You worked together? What kind of work?"

"The same kind of work I'm doin' now," Crites said.

"And you think this Rufus Slade who is a drover for the LP is the same man?"

"I know he is the same man," Crites said. "I seen 'im."

"Is he good with a gun?"

"He's damn good."

"All right, take these two men with you," Dobson said. "Get rifles, and the three of you get up on top of the Hog Waller. When those four men come out, shoot them down."

"No," Crites said. "That damn newspaper article has got ever' one in town all riled up 'n if we somethin' like that, it will only make matters worse."

"Well, what do you suggest?"

"Rufus Slade is the best they've got," Crites said. "I'm goin' to call 'im out. If the people see me shoot him down in the street, fair and square, it'll take all the sand out of 'em."

"Can you beat him?"

"I can beat 'im."

"All right, I can see that," Dobson said. "But after you kill Slade, I want you to kill Cade McCall."

"McCall ain't nobody I've ever heard of, so he can't be that much of a threat. Tisdale wasn't all that good, and when McCall killed him, he just got lucky."

"Nevertheless, I want Cade McCall dead."

25

RUFUS SAW CRITES in the mirror the moment the chief of Dobson's private police pushed through the batwing doors.

"Hello, Enos," he said calmly. He didn't turn around.

"Rufus," Crites replied just as calmly.

"It's been a long time," Rufus said. "Where was it? El Paso? Corpus Christi?"

"Laredo," Crites said.

"Oh, yes, Laredo. You sold your gun to a man named Fentress, as I recall."

"He paid more."

"He was on the wrong side," Rufus said.

"There are no sides. There's just money."

Rufus turned away from the bar to face Crites. "Where are we going to do this?" he asked.

"Outside, in the street," Crites said. "Your friend there has got folks to thinkin' maybe they don't need the services the colonel provides them. I'm goin' to kill you in front of the whole town to show them they're wrong."

"Are you insane?" Cade asked. "You can't just come in here and say you are going to kill someone."

"Are you Cade McCall?" Crites asked.

"Yes."

Crites smiled. "You're next. I don't know why, but the colonel particularly wants you dead."

"There won't be a next time for you, Enos," Rufus said.

Crites chuckled. "You always did like to make your man wonder if he would be good enough. None of 'em have been, before now. I'm good enough."

Crites turned and left the saloon.

"You're not really going out there to face him are you?" Jeter asked.

"Yes."

"Look, Rufus, I know you're good, I seen that with Shardeen," Jeter said. "But you hung up your gun a long time ago 'n Crites never did, he's been using his gun all along. Don't you think you might be a bit rusty?"

Rufus smiled. "You can buy me a drink after it's over."

"I'm going out first, just to make certain he isn't planning to shoot you as soon as you come through the door," Cade said.

"Yeah, I'm coming with you," Jeter said.

"Me too," Boo added.

When the men went outside, they saw Crites standing in the middle of Texas Street. They also saw several men from the town on the boardwalks on either side of the street. Many of the townspeople were armed.

Rufus walked out into the street and took up a position about twenty yards from Crites.

"We had some good times together," Crites said.

"Yes, we did."

"But I always knew I was better than you."

Rufus turned in such a way as to present himself to Crites in profile. "Prove it," he said.

Crites pulled his pistol so fast that Cade couldn't even follow it. There was a jerk of his shoulder and the gun was in his hand. Cade's eyes had been on Crites, rather than Rufus, so he missed the fact that Rufus's draw had been even faster, he fired first.

Crites caught the ball high in his chest. He fired his own gun then, but it was just a convulsive action and the bullet went into the dirt, just before he dropped his gun and slapped his hand over his wound. He looked down in surprise as blood squirted through his fingers, turning his shirt bright red. He took two staggering steps toward Rufus, then fell to his knees. He looked up at Rufus.

"How'd you do that?" he asked in surprise. "How'd you get your gun out that fast?" He smiled, then coughed, and flecks of blood came from his mouth. He breathed hard a couple of times. "I was sure I was faster than you."

"Looks like you were wrong," Rufus said, easily.

Crites fell face down into the street. That was when Cade saw a man on the roof of the Hog Waller. The man was pointing a rifle at Rufus.

"Rufus, look out!" Cade shouted, but even as he was calling the warning, he drew his own gun and fired. The would be assassin dropped his rifle, clasped his hands over his belly, then fell from the roof.

Immediately after that, several other shots were exchanged as both townspeople and deputies scrambled to find cover.

Rufus, who had faced Crites without a wound went down under the gunfire.

"Rufus!" Cade yelled, running toward him. Bullets zipped by him, kicking up dirt in the street.

"You were faster than Crites. I thought you said fast didn't matter."

"Sometimes it does," Rufus replied. He coughed, and blood appeared in the corner of his mouth.

Another bullet hit the street near them.

"Here endeth the lesson," Rufus said. "Get out of the street."

Now the bullets were flying by so close that Cade could hear them pop as they whipped by his ear. The level of gunfire reminded him of some of the battles he had been in during the war.

Cade left Rufus then, and running out of the street dived behind a watering trough. He saw a deputy step around the corner of a building and take aim at Rufus. Cade fired first, and the deputy went down.

The gun battle was taking place between Cade, Jeter, and Boo, who were now joined by at least a dozen citizens of the town, in opposition to every one of Dobson's deputies. For the first several minutes the firing was heavy and the battle intense. Then as attrition took its toll among the deputies, it became obvious that the deputies were losing the fight.

The only deputies still alive were in the livery barn and during a pause in the shooting, a rifle with a white cloth attached to the barrel, appeared at the door.

"Stop your shootin'! We give up! We give up!"

"Come on out, Parker, and bring all your friends with you!" Billingsly called. "Hands in the air, all of you!"

Twelve men, all twelve with their hands up, came out of the barn.

"Where are the others?" someone asked.

"They're dead," Parker replied. "You done kilt 'em all except for us."

"Where are your horses?" Billingsly asked.

"They're back in the barn."

"Pete, you and some of the others go back to the barn with them to make certain they don't pick up their guns again, then put them on their horses and get them out of here. Parker?"

"Yeah?"

"If we ever see you, or anyone else from your motley crew, we will hold a trial, and then we will hang you. Have I made myself clear?" Billingsly asked.

"What about Dobson?" Parker asked.

"Don't you worry about Dobson. We'll take care of him."

All during the exchange between Billingsly and Parker, Cade was on his knees beside Rufus's prostrate form. Jeter and Boo were with him.

"How is Mr. Slade?" Billingsly asked Cade.

"He's dead," Cade replied.

Billingsly and Cade didn't knock; they just pushed the door open and went in. Dobson was taking money from the safe and putting it in a leather satchel. His back was to the door so neither Billingsly nor Cade could see the expression on his face.

"You're through, Dobson," Billingsly said.

"I'm leaving town," Dobson replied. He had not yet turned around.

There was something about Dobson that seemed familiar to Cade, and when he spoke, it was a voice he had heard before.

Dobson turned around then and seeing him, Cade gasped in surprise.

"Albert Dolan!"

"Hello, Cade," Dolan said. "How is my old friend from the Quad?"

"You know Colonel Dobson?" Billingsly asked.

"This man isn't a colonel and he never was. He was a private in the 33rd Tennessee, and a prisoner of war in the Yankee Prison at Camp Douglas. And, he is a traitor. He betrayed the rest of us, and he got a close friend killed."

"He isn't a Union colonel? That means this whole thing has been a lie from the very start, hasn't it?" Billingsly asked.

Dolan laughed, a shrill, mocking laugh. "As soon as I got here I saw that you people didn't like Rebs, so I decided to be a blue belly, and not just any blue belly, but a colonel. You Yankee bastards were so easy to fool."

"You know who we like even less? We have absolutely no regard for someone who is a coward and who would betray his own, even if the ones you betrayed were Confederates."

"What will happen to me now?" Dolan asked.

"Even though, at the moment we don't have the legal authority to do so, I think we'll convene a special court, just for you," Billingsly said. "But then, legal authority has never meant anything to you, has it? I'm not sure what the outcome of the trial will be, but I can tell you right now that all that money you have taken will go back to the city. Maybe we can use it to support a real city government and a real city marshal."

"Does the town have a jail?" Cade asked.

"No, but Mrs. Rittenhouse has a root cellar. We can hold him there until the trial starts. But I expect that after the trial we'll hang him, so havin' a jail won't be all that important."

"You know, Cade, my old friend, I have a feeling that you are responsible for all this."

"I am not your friend," Cade said.

"Here's the money, Cade. I'll let you be the hero," Dolan said, handing the satchel over.

As cade reached for the satchel, a Derringer suddenly appeared in Dolan's hand.

"Cade, he has a gun!"

Cade shoved the satchel back toward Dolan and, taking advantage of his disorientation, drew his own pistol and fired. Both Dolan's Derringer and the money bag fell to the floor.

"You . . . you've killed me," Dolan said.

"And just when everything was going so well for you," Cade said, stepping back as Dolan collapsed.

Eighteen men had started north with Colonel Puckett, fifteen men were going back to Texas. Except for Old Rudy and Blaze, the two guide steers, they had no cattle to deal with, so the trip back was considerably faster than the trip up had been, the outfit returning to Jackson county within twenty days.

Once they were back home Puckett gave a bonus to the men who had signed on only for the drive, and gave a week off to the men who were his full time cowboys. He invited Cade and Jeter into his library, telling them that he would like to have a few words with them.

"You two men did a wonderful job for me," he said. "I watched the way you handled the IIIX herd, and the way you reacted during the stampede."

"Thanks," Cade and Jeter replied.

"This was my last trail drive. I'm too old to go through it again. So I'm offering you two an opportunity."

"You want us to take up your next herd for you?" Cade asked.

"Yes, but it involves a little more than that. I think you boys should become drive contractors. As a contractor you would make all the arrangements, you hire the men, you buy the supplies, you schedule the drive, choose the route, deal with any problems in between, and when you reach Abilene . . . or wherever you wind up, you will make the deal with the cattle broker, or the buyer."

"That's quite a responsibility," Cade said.

"Yes, it is," Colonel Puckett said. "But you will be paid very well for that responsibility. Two dollars and fifty cents per cow, and that will be free and clear. I will pay all the expenses. What do you think about that?"

"Let me ask you something, Colonel. Would you have any objection to Jeter and me rounding up some of our own cows, and taking them up with your herd, just as we did with the IIIX cows this time?"

Colonel Puckett chuckled. "You do plan to register your own brand before the next drive, don't you?"

"Yes, sir, and I've already got the brand figured out," Cade said. "It will be the MW....but with the M on top of the W. We'll only need one branding iron, all you have to do is turn it upside down."

"Welcome to the cattle business, boys," Colonel Puckett said, extending his hand.

Galveston, Texas

"Here's your money," Arabella said. "Fourteen hundred and twenty-seven dollars, which is exactly the amount of money I took from you. You can take your money and walk away, or, you could leave it as an investment."

"What sort of an investment?"

"Why, in the Red House, of course."

"How much of the Red House would fourteen hundred and twenty-seven dollars buy me?"

"One fourth?"

"How about I double that for one half?"

"You want to own half of the Red House?"

"Yes. We can use the money to make improvements."

"What sort of improvements?"

"I think we could build on an addition that would add to the number of rooms. And we could have indoor plumbing, with a lavatory in each room," Cade suggested.

"Oh, that would be marvelous!" Arabella said. "Why we could raise the rent and keep the place full."

"I thought you might like the idea."

"Do you know what I like most of all?" Arabella asked as, with a smile, she reached up to lay her hand on Cade's cheek. "I like the idea of you being my partner, and being here with me to help me run the place."

"Oh, Arabella, I can't do that. I've made other commitments that I'll have to honor in order to get established in the cattle business."

"You mean you expect me to run this alone?"

"I'm sure it will bring in enough money for you to hire some help. And, in addition to your percentage of the profit, I would expect you to pay yourself a salary, since you'll be working here, and I won't."

"All right," Arabella said. "I wish you would be here with me but . . ."

"Oh, I will be here," Cade said, interrupting her. "I intend to live here as long as I am in Galveston."

"Oh?" Arabella said, brightening. "And how long will that be?"

"I'll be here until next spring, when Jeter and I will start rounding up mavericks for our herd."

"So you plan to take a room?"

"Yes."

"That would be a foolish waste of a room, wouldn't it? I mean, if you take a room, that will just be a room that we can't rent." She smiled. "On the other hand, I already have a room."

Long Road to Abilene

Epilogue

Twin Creek Ranch, Howard County, Texas – 1927:

OWEN WISTER TYPED the last word, then rolled the platen up to remove the page and put it, face-down on the pile of papers that lay just to the right of the typewriter. He turned the pile right side up so he could see the title THE WESTERN ADVENTURES OF CADE MCCALL. He was finished, and picking the manuscript up, he held it, feeling its heft.

There was always something deeply satisfying about holding four hundred typed, and double-spaced pages. Here, in his hand, was an entire world, recreated tone and tint so that readers now, and one hundred years from now, would be able to leave their own time and place, and enter the world he, Owen Wister, had created.

"Mr. Wister?"

"Amanda," Wister replied, greeting Cade's granddaughter.

"Mama said dinner is ready if it is convenient for you to come now."

Smiling, Wister held up the manuscript. "It is most convenient now," he said.

"Are you going to let me read it?" Cade asked over the dinner table.

"Yes, of course. It's your story, after all. At least, what I have told so far."

"So far?"

"Cade, your life is the quintessential American story, our struggles, our ambitions, our defeats and our victories. I have only begun to tell it, there is much to come."

"You mean you intend to write more?"

"Yes, if you will allow another visit, I would like to come back to continue the saga."

About the Author

Robert Vaughan sold his first book when he was 19. That was 57 years and nearly 500 books ago. He wrote the novelization for the mini series *Andersonville*. Vaughan wrote, produced, and appeared in the History Channel documentary Vietnam Homecoming. His books have hit the NYT bestseller list seven times. He has won the Spur Award, the PORGIE Award (Best Paperback Original), the Western Fictioneers Lifetime Achievement Award, received the Readwest President's Award for Excellence in Western Fiction, is a member of the American Writers Hall of Fame and is a Pulitzer Prize nominee. Vaughn is also a retired army officer, helicopter pilot with three tours in Vietnam. And received the Distinguished Flying Cross, the Purple Heart, The Bronze Star with three oak leaf clusters, the Air Medal for valor with 35 oak leaf clusters, the Army Commendation Medal, the Meritorious Service Medal, and the Vietnamese Cross of Gallantry.

Find more great titles by Robert Vaughan and Wolfpack Publishing at http://wolfpackpublishing.com/robert-vaughan/

Made in the USA
Monee, IL
21 June 2020

34258530R00134